I0601406

Penthouse Variations on

anal

Penthouse Variations on

anal

BY THE EDITORS OF
PENTHOUSE VARIATIONS

Copyright ©2016 by Penthouse Global Media, Inc.

All rights reserved. Except for brief passages quoted in newspaper, magazine, radio, television or online reviews, no part of this book may be reproduced in any form or by any means, electronic or mechanical, including photocopying, recording, or information storage or retrieval system, without permission in writing from the Publisher.

Published in the United States by Cleis Press, an imprint of Start Midnight, LLC, 101 Hudson Street, 37th Floor, Suite 3705, Jersey City, NJ 07302.

Cover design: Scott Idleman/Blink
Cover photograph: iStock
Text design: Frank Wiedemann
First Edition.
10 9 8 7 6 5 4 3 2 1

Trade paper ISBN: 978-1-62778-196-1
E-book ISBN: 978-1-62778-197-8

Certain materials herein were previously published in *Penthouse Variations* magazine.

PENTHOUSE, VARIATIONS, the PENTHOUSE VARIATIONS logo, and the One Key logo are trademarks of General Media Communications, Inc., and are used by permission.

CONTENTS

Introduction

Depending on which anal aficionado you ask, backdoor sex is either an irresistible erotic taboo or just another way to play. Readers of *Penthouse Variations* magazine confess that it's one of their favorite sensual pastimes, and their adventures are reflected in the twenty torrid tales in this collection.

Curious backdoor virgins are well represented in these stories, documenting their incursion into unexplored territory with all of the excitement, apprehension, and ecstasy that goes along with giving in. Sloane Russell describes those undeniable cravings in "Asking for It":

Every time Paul had ever suggested we try anal, I had gotten wetter than I could imagine. He knew this, too. We'd be making out, and he'd say, "I want to fuck you everywhere. I want to fuck your mouth, your cunt, your ass." And I'd squirm and sigh, and yet…whenever we got to the place where we might, to that precipice where he had the lube and he had the will, I would shake my head. "It'll hurt," I'd say. "I'll be gentle," he'd promise. But no, I'd always beg off, always say, "Another time."

Our sex life was rocking hard, regardless of the fact that I did not let him be my backdoor man—until now.…

I was the one to guide the head of his cock to my rear hole. I was the one to apply the pressure, so that the head gradually widened this tightest of openings. Paul was the one to sigh as his cock slowly stretched me and gradually entered.…

I could not believe how good it felt. And then Paul did something to make it feel even better. He reached around and started to play with my clit, even as he was fucking my ass.

Longtime kinky lovers also reveal their no-holds-barred couplings, like the bold couple in Joline Jackson's "Bayou Heat":

I felt the juice seeping from my cunt. Breathless with anticipation, I waited for the moment I'd feel the big, meaty head of Tanner's cock between the globes of my ass, pressing insistently against my back door. Two seconds later, his hands were on my cheeks, spreading them apart to better expose my tiny hole. The time had come. Tanner gripped my hips, positioned his shaft between my buttocks, and deftly entered my tight orifice.

But women aren't the only lovers of anal penetration in this anthology, with men getting as good as they give. Sandy Baxter shares a tale of pegging fantasies fulfilled in "Mistress's Surprise":

> *Getting into position as instructed, Eric hovered above the dildo and then slowly lowered his ass onto it.*
>
> *"Take it all the way in," I commanded, seeing a host of emotions flash over his face as he obeyed me: lust, embarrassment, passion. "I want you to feel it all the way up to the hilt. Balls-deep. And then I want you to slide your ass up and down. If you get it right, I'll make you come like a rocket."*
>
> *As Eric followed my instructions and shamelessly took his pleasure from the toy strapped to my pelvis, I began massaging his cock and balls. My husband's movements made the base of the dildo press against the top of my slit, and the pressure teased my lust-swollen clit. My arousal spiraled upward as he rode my cock with wild abandon.*

Whether you're titillated by the taboo or are an avid anal fan, enjoy these carnal confessions about lovers who dare to follow their desires.

Barbara Pizio
Executive Editor, *Penthouse Variations*

Asking for It

SLOANE RUSSELL

"Don't forget to thank Paul," Marcia reminded me.

"I would never forget that!"

"You remember that actress who forgot to thank her husband? Well, they ended up getting a divorce."

"They were having problems anyway, remember? Drugs, I think. And infidelity."

"Still."

I fiddled with the ribbons on the front of my pink chiffon dress. I'd thought the bouffant style looked chic when I bought it. On second look, the strapless wonder appeared more like a naughty prom-night reject. What had I been thinking? There was far too much fabric, lace, and ribbons, but it was too late. Besides, it wasn't as if I were up for an Oscar. This was simply a little award benefit for the people in my field. The paparazzi wouldn't be taking my picture. There would be no red carpet.

"Do you have your speech?"

I patted my chest.

"What does that mean? You've got it written on your bra?"

"I'm not wearing a bra."

"On your chest, then?"

"I have the speech tucked into my dress," I said between clenched teeth.

"You're going to reach your hand into your bodice and pull out your list? And not expose yourself? Good luck."

If I hadn't been nervous enough already, Marcia seemed determined to send me over the edge.

"Who knows if I'll even win," I said.

"You're going to win, and then you're going to stick your hand in your dress and pull out a tit instead of your speech."

"Guess what? You're not helping." I pushed her out of my bedroom, telling her I'd talk to her later, and tried to relax. The next knock on the door made me bark, "Go away."

Paul opened the door and looked in at me.

"You're that calm, then?"

I grimaced. "I like being in back of things. I don't like being front row center."

"I know."

"What if I trip? What if I forget how to speak? And then Marcia's telling me if I forget to thank you, you'll divorce me."

"That's not what I'll do."

I gazed at him.

Paul gave me a half-smile, and then stroked my dark curls off my forehead. Even though I'd been to the hairdresser earlier in the day, my riot of curls was already mussed. "If you forget to thank me, I won't divorce you." He paused for emphasis. "I'll simply sodomize you."

Paul has always wanted to have anal sex with me, and I've always declined. Too scared. Too confused. Too something. But deep down inside, I've wondered what sex like that would feel like, and the mere thought of it turned me on.

My face flushed. I felt the heat traveling from my cheeks all the way down my throat. Paul didn't seem to notice.

"Grab your coat and let's head to the car," he said evenly.

We'd been together for seven years. Paul had tied me up. We had played with sex toys. He'd tickled me one time until I'd begged for mercy, and that had made him harder than hard. But every time he'd suggested we try doing it in the back door, I'd balked. I don't know what had scared me the most. I'd felt too vulnerable to let him do that to me.

But now, I must admit, I found the concept unexpectedly intriguing. More than that, the idea gave me something to focus on other than walking onto a stage in front of too many people.

"I'll be right there," I said. After he left, I pulled out my speech and threw the paper in the trash can. Quickly, I wrote out a brand-new speech and tucked the paper into my sweetheart neckline. Feeling much calmer, I lifted my velvet cape off the back of my chair, wrapped the plush fabric around my shoulders, and trailed after Paul.

Had his sexy threat steeled my nerves? I can't say. All I know is that I managed the evening with ease, holding on to Paul's arm, nodding at every compliment I received. I mingled with the other guests before settling into my seat at Paul's side.

He was the epitome of the supportive husband. Paul's work is conducted mostly in boardrooms. He doesn't usually mix with creative types. So this was a dazzling event for him, but he didn't have any reason to feel left out or jealous. He's successful in his own right and was happy to encourage my career.

I think I went into some sort of trance for the majority of the event. I watched the different nominees accept their prizes. I listened to the speeches. I mentally rehearsed my own in my head.

"I'd like to thank…"

Finally, the nominees for the award in my category were announced. Paul gripped my knee. I closed my eyes. "And the winner is…"

"It's going to be you," Paul whispered in my ear.

"Sloane Russell."

I felt a wave of fear ripple through me as Paul said, "Get up, baby. Go get your prize."

Then I remembered what he'd said back at home, and I steadied myself and walked up the stairs to the stage. The speech I pulled from my dress was written in shaky handwriting. I squinted, but I could hardly see the words, let alone read them. Still, I managed to thank everyone I wanted to. By the time I returned to Paul, my heart had stopped racing at triple-speed, and I felt calm and at ease. Paul, however, had a look in his eyes.

"The limo's waiting," he said. There was a chill in his tone that excited me.

I let him lead me through the crowd, let him help me into the backseat. I felt my nerves jangling, but for a different reason entirely.

Paul held my hand and stroked my fingertips. He leaned against me and kissed my neck, then my chest. "We're not going to do *that* in the limo," I murmured.

"You're right," he whispered to me. "The lube's at home."

I don't know why his words made me so wet, but I was shifting in my seat, desperate for us to get back to our house. Fuck the after parties, I wanted Paul to fuck *me*, and in a way that he never had. Clearly, Paul wanted that, too. But first we had to do something—something to cut the tension, something to take the edge off.

"Tell me what it's going to be like," I begged.

"Oh, Sloane. I've wanted to fuck your asshole for years. I can hardly stand to wait another minute."

I looked down. His pants were tented with his erection. I bent over and kissed him through his slacks. His hand found the back of my hair, started pushing my lips harder against him.

"Tell me," I murmured.

"You keep doing that."

I undid his button, and then pulled down his zipper. I released his cock and started to suck while Paul verbally painted a pretty picture of all things anal. "First, I'm going to strip you out of that silly dress and stand you up in front of me. I want to look at you, touch you, get on my knees behind you and stroke your gorgeous ass."

I bobbed up and down. I didn't care what the driver thought. I couldn't stop myself. Hunger had stoked my libido to an extreme.

"Then I'm going to part your pretty cheeks and peek at your asshole."

The thought of him looking at me there, of viewing me so

intimately, made me feel shaky. But it also made my pussy clench. I was more turned on than I wanted to admit. Luckily, I didn't have to admit anything at all—not with my mouth stuffed full of Paul's cock. Paul reached around and hiked up my dress. In seconds, he had his hand in my panties, and he knew for himself exactly how aroused I was.

"You like the thought," he insisted. "You like knowing that as soon as we get home, you're going to lose your anal virginity. I am going to go where no man—or toy—has ever gone before."

I'd never thought about the situation like that, and suddenly I was even more excited. We were going to do something brand-new. After seven years. How many couples can make that claim?

"I can't wait to feel how tight you are," he whispered. "It's going to be so sexy, Sloane. Your asshole contracting around my cock."

I couldn't wait either. Without a word, I pulled my lips off Paul and spun around so I could sit on his lap, facing him. I slid aside my little panties and lowered myself onto his rod. Paul was the one to sigh now. I squeezed him in effortless rhythm, imagining that he was fucking my asshole the whole time.

"What are you thinking about, Sloane?"

How did he know exactly when to ask a question like that?

"You know," I whispered.

"Tell me."

"You fucking me there."

"Where?"

My face was as pink as my dress. I could feel fuchsia in my cheeks, on my neck.

"Say it."

"Don't make me."

He stopped thrusting. I bit my lip. I wanted him to do it. I'm not lying. All I could think about was him getting me home and doing exactly what he'd described: undressing me, then inspecting me, and then fucking my ass. But saying the words did something strange to my head—they made the vision feel too real.

Paul lifted me up and pulled me off his cock. I whimpered, desperate.

"I won't fill you up again until you tell me what you want."

"Oh god, Paul."

I wondered if the limo driver knew what we were doing. Of course he did. We were doing what every set of lovers has done in a limo—or has wanted to do—since *No Way Out*. But I wondered if he could guess what we were planning on doing next, when we got home, when we had lube. For some reason, that thought elevated the moment for me. I mean, we could have been doing this anywhere: in the front seat of our car, in the backyard, on our porch. But the fact that we were in a limo—and that by nature of the beast, there was someone in close proximity to us—that made my heart race.

"Say it."

Paul wasn't letting up. Or letting me go down. He had other plans.

"I want you to fuck my ass," I said, so softly I could hardly even hear my own words.

"Louder."

"I want you to bend me over," I said, "and fuck my ass. I want you to pour on lube. I want you to make me so slippery-wet I can't stand it. And then I want you to drive your cock hard inside my back hole."

Paul moved me so that I was astride him once more, but I didn't stop talking. I couldn't stop talking.

"That's all I could think of when I took the stage tonight," I confessed. "What you were going to do with me when we got home."

Paul sighed, "Me, too. I saw you up on stage, and in my head, you were naked, bent over, parting your rear cheeks with your fingers for me."

"And you imagined fucking my ass up there, with everyone watching."

"Yeah," he groaned. "Oh god, Sloane. I'm so close."

He slid one hand in between our bodies and let his fingertips crest over my clit. I was so swollen and ripe and ready that I started to come with that light touch. But Paul wasn't satisfied with only touching me with his fingers. He stroked me with his words. "It's going to feel so good, Sloane. You're going to come so hard."

"I am," I said—both telling him what was happening right then, and agreeing with his assessment for the future.

When we got home, we didn't spend any time even pretending we were done for the night. Exactly as he had when we were newlyweds, he hoisted me in his arms and carried me to our bedroom. "Do you like that dress?" he asked.

"Well..." I didn't really. It was a deflated prom dress. But I wanted to keep the thing for memory's sake.

"Better take it off, then."

I unzipped and stripped as Paul headed into our bathroom. He returned with a bottle of lube. Then he left the room once more, coming back with a bottle of champagne and two glasses.

While I watched, he popped the bubbly and poured us each a flute.

"To celebrate," he said.

"My win?"

"Or something…"

I took the champagne with a shaking hand. Paul helped me sip from the glass, and then he set the flute back on the bedside table.

"Are you ready?"

"I don't think so."

"Let me help."

He spread me out on our comforter and began to run his palms over my body. I started to let myself relax. He added a drop of the lubricant to his hands and then spread the glossy liquid all over my skin. I was nearly humming with pleasure by the time he reached the curves of my ass. I sucked in my breath. Was he going to spread my cheeks open? Was he going to let his fingertips dart between them? I have to admit, I wanted him to. It was something we'd never done before—not because of Paul, but because of me. I'd been scared. That's the truth. But I'd also been secretly aroused.

Every time Paul had ever suggested we try anal, I had gotten wetter than I could imagine. He knew this, too. We'd be making out, and he'd say, "I want to fuck you everywhere. I want to fuck your mouth, your cunt, your ass." And I'd squirm and sigh, and yet…whenever we got to the place where we might, to that precipice where he had the lube and he had the will, I would shake my head. "It'll hurt," I'd say. "I'll be gentle," he'd promise. But no, I'd always beg off, always say, "Another time."

Our sex life was rocking hard, regardless of the fact that I did not let him be my backdoor man—until now.

But he wasn't even trying. He massaged my thighs, my calves, my feet, then worked himself back up my body. Why wasn't he touching my ass? I raised my hips. I lifted myself off the bed. All he had to do was spread me open like a piece of ripe fruit. I knew somehow exactly what that would feel like—his cockhead at the opening he'd never entered before. There'd be pressure, but he'd go slowly. I'd close my eyes. I'd breathe quickly. I'd relax and let him in.

Yet where was he? I'll tell you where. He was rolling me over and caressing my breasts. Then he was kissing in a line down my neck, touching my hips, my waist, the tender skin on the insides of my thighs. Jesus fucking Christ, why was he *not* fucking my ass?

It took every ounce of reserve on my part not to start begging. And then I realized—I can be slow—begging was what Paul wanted. As he continued to run the palms of his large hands over my body, I wriggled in his embrace. Once more, I positioned myself facedown on the bed. I butted against Paul. I pressed my ass to his groin, and I whispered, "Fuck me."

Paul started to slide his cock into my pussy. I wanted to say, "Not my cunt, you idiot. My ass!" But then I accepted how good this felt, and I thought, *Okay. Get nice and wet with my pussy juice. And then you can take my ass.* He rode me sweetly, his cock hitting all those secret places within me, pressing hard, grinding deep. I felt the pleasure begin to build. Paul gripped me and held on tight, then swiveled his hips so his cock seemed to grow even larger within me. Suddenly, I felt a little worried. Would I be able to take a cock this large in my ass?

One thing was for sure—I wanted to find out.

Without a word, I pulled forward. Paul tried to hold me back, but I moved away. His cock was free from my body. Paul didn't say a word. I reached back and gripped the shaft. Paul groaned.

"I want you to fuck me," I said softly. "Not my pussy. Not my mouth. I want you to fuck my ass."

"You really want that?"

"Yes, Paul."

"Show me."

I was the one to guide the head of his cock to my rear hole. I was the one to apply the pressure, so that the head gradually widened this tightest of openings. Paul was the one to sigh as his cock slowly stretched me and gradually entered.

"Slow," I said, breathless, as he drizzled lube down my asscrack.

"Slow," he said back to me, slipping in a millimeter at a time.

I'd never felt anything like that. The fullness, the satisfaction of having something inside me, *there*. My pussy was a lake of wetness in response. I could hardly think or speak or move. Paul took over, seeming to understand. He held my hips and gently, perfectly slid inside me. Once he was in, he stayed like that, sealed to me, until I said, "Now. I'm ready. Fuck me."

That's all he needed to hear. Because then he was in motion, fucking my ass in long, even strokes. I could not believe how good it felt. And then Paul did something to make it feel even better. He reached around and started to play with my clit, even as he was fucking my ass.

"Oh," I moaned. "Oh please."

"You like that."

"So much."

"Tell me how it feels."

"Like being split open, but filled at the same time."

Paul sighed.

He kept driving inside me, fucking my asshole as if he were fucking my pussy. I could tell when he started to reach his limit, could tell by the change in his breathing, the speed of the ride. "I'm almost there," he said.

"Do it," I begged. "Come inside me."

That's all he needed to hear. He bucked and then stiffened, and I felt him climaxing within me. Even as he was lost in his own orgasm, he managed to trick his fingers up and over my clit. His magic fingertips danced up and over again and again, until I came with him, fiercely and powerfully, taken away by the satisfaction and intensity combined.

Afterward, we showered, and then collapsed onto the bed with fresh glasses of champagne. And then I remembered—my speech. The tiny folded-up piece of paper lay on the bedside table.

"Here," I said.

Paul raised his eyebrows, then unfolded the paper and read the words aloud. "I'd like to thank Paul, my one and only love." It was a short speech.

He refolded the paper and smiled at me. And then he started to laugh.

Why had I made him wait that long? Why hadn't I realized how sexy it would feel? I didn't have an answer for that. But I did know one thing—I wasn't going to wait until I won another award before we had anal sex again.

Bayou Heat

JOLINE JACKSON

It was a sweltering day on the bayou—the kind of weather that, for some reason, always makes me horny—when I noticed that the bottle of lube on the nightstand was dangerously low. For someone who loves anal sex as much as I do, running out of lubricant is not an option. I threw on a little sundress, brushed my honey-blonde hair, and turned to my hubby. "Tanner," I said, "I need a few things from the store."

He was working on the evap cooler in the bedroom window. The device had quit overnight, leaving Tanner and me with sticky sheets by morning. Tanner is great with machines—he's got a classic muscle car that he's nearly finished restoring—but so far he hadn't been able to fix the cooler.

Sweaty and irresistibly sexy in his boxer shorts, Tanner turned and said, "Okay, babe. Maybe I'll have this fixed by the time you get back."

I kissed him; he pulled me close and kissed me back, running his hand up my bare thigh. I felt my ardor rise and thought of pulling him to the bed, but then I remembered the lube situation. Extricating myself, I said, "I won't be long."

My destination was the adult superstore some twenty miles away, where I bought a bottle of anal grease, plus three pairs of sexy thong underwear that had caught my eye. When I got back home, the twang of Tanner's acoustic guitar led me to the carport, which sat well back from the street. The muggy air was perfectly still; in seconds, my dress stuck to my skin as I walked up the rutted gravel track. I didn't mind, though. Like I said, there's something about sultry weather that turns me on—and boy, was it working that day!

Barefoot and bare-chested, Tanner sat on a stool beside his car, plucking a melancholy tune. Grease smudges decorated his arms and chest. "Hey, Jo," he said, putting the guitar down.

"Jesus, it's like a sauna out here," I said, fanning myself with my free hand. In the other, I held my bag of goodies from the store.

"Even worse in the house," Tanner said. "Need a part for the evap. I called around. Soonest I can get it is the day after tomorrow."

"Well, never mind that. I have a few things to show you." I kicked off my flip-flops, then unzipped my dress and stepped out of it, grabbing Tanner's undivided attention in the process. The car—not to mention the big shrubs growing along the curb out front—shielded us from passersby. I don't wear a bra, because my small breasts are really perky. So, when I slid my panties off, I was completely nude. Tanner's eyebrows went up and a grin spread across his face.

"Now, what do you think of these?" I asked, taking one of the new pairs of panties from the bag and putting them on. After giving him a good look at the front, I turned around to show him the back. Tanner always says my derriere is my best feature, and I know my cheeky display revved him up big-time. I was feeling mighty aroused myself, and as I modeled the other two thongs for him, I really got into it, shaking my behind in his face and bending over like a strip-club dancer. Tanner loved it. He caressed my asscheeks with his calloused hands, and I could feel the want in his touch.

I removed the last thong and tossed it back in the bag. When I turned to face him again, I was not surprised to see the outline of a bulging erection in his jeans. "Oh, Tanner," I said, sitting astride one of his knees. The denim felt warm and pleasantly rough against my bare cunt. I began thrusting my pelvis to and fro, just an inch or two—enough to rub my clit smartly against him. White-hot sparks of excitement shot through my body.

Tanner kissed me passionately. His arms were around me, but he seemed to be holding back from touching me the way he wanted to. "Baby," he started, "I got grease all over me."

"The only grease that matters right now is *this*," I declared, leaning over to grab the bottle of lube.

Tanner took it from me and kissed me again, so fiercely that my heart beat double-time. I stood up to let him free his cock. He pulled his jeans and underwear down and stood before me, enjoying my stare. His prick never fails to amaze me. Long and thick, it stood straight out from his groin like a billy club. I couldn't wait to feel it driving deep into my ass.

Tanner glanced over at the house and said, "Too damn hot in there."

Before the words were out of his mouth, I bent over the red-striped hood of his car and planted my feet well apart on the concrete slab. "Here, fuck me here!" I demanded.

Tanner whistled with appreciation. Quickly, he got into position behind me and oiled up his monster rod. Then I felt his fingers at my rear opening, massaging a dollop of the lube into my sphincter. I squirmed, enjoying the naughty feeling. He pushed his thumb in to the knuckle, then withdrew it and replaced it with two fingers. I gasped with delight and cried, "Keep going!"

Carefully, he added a third digit, and then wiggled them all around, just enough to make sure my taut ring of muscle was pliant and ready. I felt the juice seeping from my cunt. Breathless with anticipation, I waited for the moment I'd feel the big, meaty head of Tanner's cock between the globes of my ass, pressing insistently against my back door. Two seconds later, his hands were on my cheeks, spreading them apart to better expose my tiny hole. The time had come. Tanner gripped my hips, positioned his shaft between my buttocks, and deftly entered my tight orifice.

"Aaah," I groaned. "Fuck, oh fuck—that feels good." As Tanner leaned into me, propelling his tool farther up my back passage, he placed his palm against the small of my back and urged me to lie flat against the car's hood. I pressed my boobs and belly to the painted metal surface and found that the new angle of Tanner's dick in my butt was better than ever.

"You've got such a pretty ass," Tanner said as he bottomed out inside me. "Such a perfect, tight ass." His ball sac smacked against my cunt lips, sending extra shivers of delight through my body. He stroked my butt with adoration, while he withdrew his cock almost all the way, then slid in completely again. I moaned at the onslaught of intense pleasure and pushed back at him, desperate for more.

"I love that you love this," he added, pumping faster now. "I love that you can't get enough of my cock in your ass…because I can't, either." He thrust harder still, pummeling away at my rump so ardently that the car began to rock beneath me. My whole body was slick with perspiration, and that made me slide against the metal surface like a slippery eel.

"That's it!" I cried, feeling my pleasure cresting. I extended my arms and grabbed hold of the hood, just below the windshield wipers. "Oh god—that's it." I couldn't say anything more for a while after that, except meaningless gibberish, as I undulated against the car.

Tanner kept a good grip on my hips and kept sawing in and out of my ass until I regained a measure of control, then he pulled out and asked me to turn over. Curious to see what he had in mind, I lay flat on my back against the hood and lifted my feet to the fender. With a sly wink, he parted my knees wide, and then he lowered his head to my pussy. His tongue, strong and wet, darted between the lips of my sex and slid within my sopping folds. Tanner began lapping up my juices as if he were parched. At the same time, he pushed two fingers between my asscheeks and started working them in and out of my back door. A shriek of pleasure escaped my lips, and my back arched involuntarily off the car, so intense were the sensations I was experiencing. I stared up at the roof of the carport and struggled not to howl; the last thing we needed at that moment was to draw the attention of the neighbors. At any rate, it was only a minute or two longer before Tanner had me coming. I grabbed my breasts and gave in to a series of wild tremors, which made my ass bounce against the hood.

I was still trembling with postorgasmic bliss as Tanner straightened up, resupplied his shaft with lube, and stuffed it into my ass once more. He felt incredibly big back there, and yet I wanted it all, every inch of him inside me. He was right: I couldn't get enough. Tanner was just as enthusiastic. He moved in and out of my fanny with incredible vigor, completely filling me with every thrust. I put my legs up over his shoulders, and he held my knees while he plundered my tush in earnest. Beneath me, the car rocked crazily, and the shocks squeaked in protest, but the brakes held.

"Oh, baby, here it comes," Tanner growled through clenched teeth. The muscles in his arms and chest tightened, as did his grip on my legs. He rammed his cock in and out of my ass half a dozen times more, and then his dick erupted, filling my tight passage with semen. Again and again he spasmed inside me, until at last he collapsed on top of me. His dick slipped out of my rear end, followed by some of his semen. We were both sweating profusely, but we were content to lie there for a while.

Eventually, Tanner and I went inside for a long, cool shower. "Good thing you bought that lube," my husband said as he soaped my breasts. "We're going to need more of it tomorrow."

I figured that was true, since I was already looking forward to our next round of play, but Tanner seemed to have something specific in mind. "What's tomorrow?" I asked.

He had a mischievous twinkle in his eye, which piqued my interest. "The fish fry at that restaurant, remember?"

"Oh, yeah." The occasion was supposed to include live music and dancing. We'd promised the friend of a friend that we would go, but we weren't likely to know many people there. I knew what Tanner was thinking. He wanted us to slip away at some point during the event for some illicit anal fun.

With that exciting notion on both our minds, we went to the restaurant the following afternoon. The food wasn't bad, but the live band left much to be desired, and we hardly knew a soul. At least the place was air-conditioned—a good thing, since the weather was still hot and sticky. After a few beers and one dance, Tanner took me by the hand and led me down a hall opposite the kitchen.

"Where are we going?" I asked, laughing. I had my answer a moment later, as Tanner pushed open the door to the unisex bathroom. It was small—one stall, a sink, and a scratched-up mirror—but it would suffice for our purposes. I locked the door and turned to Tanner, who was already lowering his jeans. His lovely cock stood proud and tall—ready for action.

"Someone's turned on," I said with a smirk, as I knelt down in front of him. The floor was a little grimy, not too bad, but I didn't really care as I lowered my mouth over Tanner's hefty stick. The sheer girth of his shaft forced my lips to form a wide circle. "Mmm," I moaned, enjoying the size and taste of him. I had just eaten dinner, of course, but I was still plenty hungry for cock. Tanner held my head lightly between his hands and uttered a quiet, heartfelt moan as I bobbed back and forth. His dick throbbed against my tongue, its fat crown leaking precome into my throat. Soon I would feel that monstrous shaft slide into my bottom, expanding my very soul as it took me to new heights. My breath quickened at the thought, and I sat back, feeling almost dizzy with desire.

"Sit up here," Tanner said, slapping the white, square sink. He was a little short of breath, after the oral attention I'd just given him.

I perched on the edge of the sink with my knees wide and flipped up my skirt. Since I'd taken off my underwear before we left the house, he had an unfettered view of my private parts. "Beautiful," he murmured, staring at my wispy blonde pubic hair like he'd never seen it before. His reaction increased my lust, and I spread my glistening-wet pussy lips apart, offering him a graphic view of my pink recesses. He lowered his head at once and started eating me with gusto.

Someone tried to open the bathroom door, cursed, and stomped off. "Fuck yeah," was all I could say as Tanner, licking voraciously, kept his face pressed firmly against my dripping sex. I was eager to feel his tongue in my ass, too, so I lifted my feet all the way to the sink and leaned back against the mirror. Tanner got the message instantly. He slid his tongue down along my perineum to my tiny hole and explored the rim for a moment, then nudged inside.

I was thrilled by the wicked feeling. He tongued my ass zealously and rubbed his thumb against my clit at the same time, making me moan and squirm. I coiled my fingers in his hair and held his head tightly to my favorite pleasure zone as my climax swept through me. Somehow I managed not to fall off the sink.

When my sanity returned, I was more desperate than ever for some serious anal fucking. Hopping down to the floor, I turned my backside to Tanner and grabbed the sink with both hands, then bent over and pushed my butt out behind me. "Lube's in my purse," I said over my shoulder, but Tanner had already retrieved it. I waggled my hips impatiently while he finished coating his shaft with the slippery liquid. He wasn't going to rush things, though. I knew he was enjoying the sight of my ass jutting out toward him, the two pale globes slightly spread, with my glistening pussy just below. The mirror was only a few inches away from my face. I looked at myself in the scratched, pitted glass, and the face that looked back at me was flushed with lust.

An instant later, Tanner slid his prick between the cheeks of my rump and pushed into my eager hole. He took his time, impaling me slowly to maximize his pleasure and mine. At last, his hips met my fanny and his balls touched my labia. I was packed completely full back there, stuck tight on my husband's dick. "Jesus, that's deep," I said, breathing out a long sigh of pleasure. Tanner eased out, nudged his cock's head against my back door again, and shoved in once more, harder this time. I grunted, feeling tingles of extreme pleasure flowing out from my core. I loved the dirty, taboo feeling of being taken like this, in the ass from behind—and in a grungy restaurant bathroom, no less. "Fuck me harder," I pleaded to Tanner. "Fuck my ass as hard as you can!"

My raunchy appeal ignited a frenzy of desire in my husband. He clamped his hands on my shoulders and rocked his cock in and out of my butt with desperate passion. I gripped the sink tighter, and it creaked against its moorings, but I doubt we'd have stopped what we were doing even if the grubby thing had fallen off the wall. I was so attuned to the feel of Tanner's penis ramming into my deepest, darkest passage that I barely heard the next rattle of the door handle, nor the subsequent knocking. Whoever it was would have to wait. Tanner's thrusts had become short and lightning quick; we were nearing the endgame. His crown never tarried near my sphincter now, remaining instead within the depths of my behind while the base of his shaft pistoned through my anus like a machine.

All this fierce fucking was pressing my cunt against the sink's edge, and my clit responded, turning my inner folds all slick and gooey.

I reached down and toggled my swollen button between my fingers until I could only gasp for breath.

"Baby, I'm gonna come," Tanner growled. I felt his body tense, and his grip on my shoulders tightened. The spasmodic thrusts of his hips drove his cock into my ass as deep as it could go and mashed my clit against my fingers at the same time. Waves of unspeakable pleasure shook me to the core, and moments later, Tanner cried out his release. His dick spasmed wildly inside my rear end; I felt his jism spray inside me hotly. He lowered his hands to my hips and kept thrusting until we were both totally spent.

When we finally exited the bathroom, a couple of people were waiting in the hall outside. The looks on their faces were priceless. We headed straight out to our car and drove off into the humid evening with our windows down. Before we got home, I was already dreaming up scenarios for our next naughty encounter.

Man of Teal

EMILIE PARIS

"What were you guys up to today?" Ben asked Mack.

"Uh, buying new clothes," my guy answered as he rummaged through his shiny silver toolbox.

"She sucked you into shopping on a Saturday?" Ben groaned, shooting a disparaging look in my direction.

"I didn't mind," Mack said quickly. "It wasn't that bad."

"What sort of clothes?" Ben asked, as if maybe we'd been shopping for something cool, like a leather jacket.

"Dressy," Mack responded without flinching.

I was doing the dishes, and I had to look away so I didn't laugh out loud. By "dressy," he definitely meant *dress*-y. But I was pretty secure in the knowledge that my husband was not planning on telling all to our neighbor. Ben let the conversation go, and after borrowing the hammer he'd stopped by for, he left through the back door. Mack sighed with relief and kicked off his boots. Now I did have to laugh, because my hubby still had on the fishnets he'd been wearing all day. He wiggled his toes at me.

Although my man is all man—nearly six feet tall, broad, and strong—he gets turned on by dressing in girly clothes. Yes, Mack is a cross-dresser, and it's one of my favorite things about him. This morning, we'd gone out shopping together. I was, for all intents and purposes, his beard. He was able to walk into all of the ladies' clothing stores by accompanying me, and the salesgirls treated him sweetly because they all assumed that he was being a dutiful husband.

They, like Ben, had no idea.

In order to keep up appearances, I made sure it looked as if I was buying clothes for a friend. I chose outfits that I knew would suit Mack, in Mack's size, but I talked constantly about whether *Mackenzie* would like what I was buying. Mack nodded and complimented all of my selections, subtly letting me know which styles he preferred. He always lets me help dress him. That's one of my other favorite parts about our relationship. Ever since we first hooked up, he's put his style into my capable hands.

That day we'd gone to several stores, and I'd chosen what could only be described as slutty clothes. Mackenzie, you see, has a much naughtier dress style than I could ever pull off. She prefers her hemlines short and to the point, at least, if the point is to catch a glimpse of the tops of her garters. Mack couldn't wait to try on the outfits, and he'd actually been pre-dressed in anticipation—with shiny satin panties dotted with cherries, those fishnet hose, and a slinky bra under his regular male clothes. He'd been about to strip when Ben had shown up unannounced, wanting to borrow a tool.

I wanted to get my hands on a tool, too. But that would have to wait.

Mack watched as I locked our back door. No more unexpected interruptions for us. Then he stripped down to those turquoise fishnets and satin bra and panties. He'd had the gear on all day, and I could tell from the rise in his panties that he'd been dealing with ever-growing arousal throughout the afternoon. He must have been dying during the conversation with Ben, wanting nothing more than for his buddy to leave.

Now, he went to the first bag and pulled out one of the dresses. Mack is a tough guy, but he's lean and wiry. He slid into the formfitting teal-colored dress without a problem. He's not naturally curvy at all, and the dress showed off his sleek physique. I helped him out by adding a sash around his waist, which emphasized how svelte he is. He then went to a second bag and pulled out a pair of boots. He's lucky to have smallish feet for a guy—a size ten, which translates to a twelve for women. He zipped himself into the patent-leather boots that were a matching hue of his dress and stockings. Then he looked at me expectantly.

"You're so fucking hot," I said. I could hardly restrain myself. When Mack begins to become Mackenzie, all I want to do is screw. But I knew how badly Mack craved the whole sensation of dressing like a girl. He was looking at me in that way because he wanted me to do the rest, to fix his hair, to add his makeup, to make the transformation complete.

"Can we go upstairs?" he asked.

"Only if you let me suck you off first."

What guy could refuse a request like that? Mack nodded, and I dropped instantly to my knees on our cool black-and-white linoleum floor. He hiked his dress up, and I cradled his cock through his satiny drawers. In seconds, the front of the panties were wet with his precome. This whole event was obviously turning Mack on to the extreme. Of course, he likes me to give him blow jobs when he's dressed in his normal clothes. But being in the feminine outfit definitely was enhancing the experience for him. I wet his panties further by licking his shaft through the fabric. I thought to myself that Ben would not believe this image if he were to interrupt us now. He'd knock on the door, or peer in the diamond-shaped window, and see me on the floor, blowing my man in drag. Although we've never had an audience, that thought turned me on even more. To control myself, I had to slip a hand between my legs to play with my pussy while I sucked on Mack's cock through the satin of his undergarments.

"Don't tease me," Mack pleaded, and I dragged his panties down his thighs, finally releasing his gorgeous hard-on. I really lost myself then, bobbing up and down on his shaft, making him slippery with my tongue. I knew he wasn't going to fuck me. Not yet. But I also knew I was going to make him shoot his load down my throat before I took him upstairs to put on his makeup. One good solid orgasm would help us both slow down and enjoy the rest of the evening.

Mack began to twist his fingers in my long hair, and I ran my palms up and down his thigh-high stockings. I'd chosen these hose for him myself. He always looks so sexy in fishnets. He keeps his legs clean-shaven for those times when we decide to play like this, and his skin felt soft and supple beneath the pattern of the stockings. The more

I touched him, the harder his cock got, until I knew he was nearing his peak. I used one hand to work the base of his dick while I hummed around the shaft. He groaned and began to fuck my face, definitely showing me who was running the show. Mack might have had a dress on, but plenty of testosterone was pumping through his veins. I pinched my clit in anticipation of his orgasm, timing my own pleasure so we came nearly simultaneously. Mack filled my mouth with his essence, while I creamed in my panties. Then we each stayed still for a moment, both of us momentarily dazed with pleasure. I'd wanted to do that all day long; I'm sure Mack felt the same way.

But in a few seconds, he'd regained his decorum and looked down at me with the same yearning expression. He was ready to be Mackenzie, not simply Mack in a dress. The difference is actually striking. Yes, I can appreciate the feminine in my man when he is dressed prettily. Yet when I sit him at my makeup table and help him do his face, the results are breathtaking for him and for me.

Now that we'd both gotten *O* number one out of the way, we could take our time and play. I followed Mack up the stairs, loving the way his legs looked in those net stockings and brand-new boots. When we reached our bedroom, he sat in his usual place and waited expectantly for me to do my magic. I pulled out my makeup kit and began going through the colors, knowing that Mack never wants me to rush. He likes me to set out the items I'm planning on using, and then ask him questions about which hues he prefers.

That night, I went for a smoky look. I asked him to choose the color palette, and once he'd landed on violet, I got busy. First, I outlined his lovely green eyes with a deep eggplant pencil. Then I swept a sparkly purple all the way up to his eyebrows. Since he's blond, he has fine brows that don't need much work from me. He can't get away with me plucking them—people like Ben would give him too much grief. So all I do is comb them with a little gadget and spread a tiny bit of gel to give them shape. Next, I went to work with my big fluffy brush, choosing a color called Breezy, which was plum with a little shimmer, and made by the perfect company for us—MAC. I saved Mack's lips for last, because I kept kissing him throughout the makeup application. But when we were done with the mascara and there was nothing else to do, I slicked on a gorgeous deep red for him and topped that with a coat of gloss. His mouth was porn-star perfect. I tied a silk scarf around his short curls, and that was all he needed.

Mack looked in the mirror, and I knew he liked what he saw when he winked at me. And in that wink, he changed. I'm not sure exactly how that works for Mack, but somehow I can always tell when Mackenzie is in the room. She turned around fully to face me, and I sucked in my breath. I'd outdone myself. She looked beautiful. For a moment, we simply stared at each other. But unlike a work of art on a museum wall, static and unbending, this was a piece of performance art. No way was I going to be a passive observer.

I held out my hand, and Mackenzie stood. I'm a tall girl, and since Mackenzie had on boots and I had on heels, we were about the same height. Now was the moment of truth. Often, when my man takes on this form, he wants something very special from me. I was about to find out if it was going to be that kind of night.

"You look lovely tonight, Mackenzie," I said, and she blushed. "You make me want to do such naughty things to you."

I kept my eyes on Mackenzie's face as I spoke, wanting to see if she'd give me a sign that I was going in the right direction.

"Like what?" she purred, her voice that husky whisper I have come to love.

"Like…" I started, and I ran my hands down Mackenzie's back and cradled her ass through her dress. She sighed and bucked against me. I knew what to do. While she sat down on the bed and watched, I stripped out of my own clothes and rummaged in the bottom drawer of my dresser, where we keep all of our toys. I felt her eyes on me as I buckled on my special harness and chose a dildo. We have a whole slew to use for different types of events. If I want my own blow job, I use a fairly realistic dildo, one that is anatomically correct. But for what I was in the mood for right now, I chose a sleek model that was slightly slimmer. Mackenzie knew exactly what that meant: I was going to take her sweet ass.

With wide eyes, Mackenzie watched as I got out a bottle of lube and slowly slicked the toy from head to base. I really spread the gel all over, wanting the toy to be nice and wet for her. Then I began to issue commands.

"Get up on your hands and knees," I told her, and she obeyed immediately. I admired her tight ass through the dress, but then told her to hike her garment to her waist. She did what I said. Because she gets so turned on by wearing panties, I didn't want to take them off. Instead, I pushed them aside, revealing her gorgeous peach of an ass and the split between her cheeks. Suddenly, I couldn't wait. Everything had to move fast. I bent down and licked in a line down the valley of her asscheeks. Mackenzie groaned loudly and bucked back, pushing her butt toward my face. I used my hands, still slippery with lube, to spread her cheeks wide and then I began to eat her asshole as if it was a pussy.

"Oh god," Mackenzie whimpered. "Oh yes. Don't stop!"

I licked in a tight circle around her hole, then began to dart the tip of my tongue deep inside. Mackenzie began to moan, and when I let one hand slide forward to stroke her cock, she started to breathe in sharp, jagged gasps.

"You like that don't you, you filthy girl," I hissed.

"Yes, I love it," she agreed. "I love when you lick me like that."

I rimmed her good, driving my face against her. I could have spent all night licking her asshole and manhandling her cock, but then I remembered the toy between my legs. With an effort, I withdrew and rose, then gripped her around the hips and pulled her into position. I let her feel the head of the toy press against her slicked-up asshole, and she started to beg me again.

"Put it in me," Mackenzie whispered. "Please, baby."

"Please what?" I wanted to hear her say the words.

"Fuck me."

Nope. Those weren't the right words. I stayed where I was, my cock poised at her hole. But I wouldn't go further. Not yet. She sensed what I was waiting for.

"Please," she tried again, "fuck my asshole. Put your cock in my ass."

When she talks like that, I sometimes imagine that we're lesbians. That she's a girl and I'm a girl, and I'm fucking her the way she likes best. Other times I pretend that we're straight but swapped. That I'm a man and she's a woman, and I use my cock to give her the exact type of pleasure she desires. I guess ultimately it doesn't really matter what story I tell myself. All that matters is that I get her off the way I crave—the way she needs.

I thrust my synthetic cock into her hole, and Mackenzie made the sweetest, happiest noises. She groaned and sighed. She actually reached back and parted her cheeks for me, so I could drive in even deeper. That touched me somehow, that submissive gesture, and I began to feel my clit swell beneath the base of the toy. Each forward buck of my hips won me electric jolts of pleasure. If I kept fucking her just right, we'd both be seeing stars.

Of course, I knew how to help us. I lubed up my right hand and began to jack Mackenzie off while I fucked her. My fist pistoned up and down the shaft of her thick cock, and she became wordless in her murmurings.

I wished I could have felt her ass contract on my dick when she came. That was the only thing missing for me. But I sensed when her release was imminent, and I tightened my fist on her and fucked her even harder. When Mackenzie climaxed, she shot her load all over the sheets. Then she went momentarily limp. I pulled out and removed the harness. She might have been done, but I wasn't.

I returned to the bed and told her to turn over. "You have to pay for your orgasm," I told her, and she looked at me with lust-filled eyes. I moved onto the bed and spread my legs. "I want you to eat me out like you never have before," I told her. "I want your tongue on me and your fingers thrusting in my pussy. Eat me like I'm your last meal."

She was in motion immediately, doing exactly what I'd instructed, bringing my legs over her shoulders and burrowing in. She started by licking my clit, sucking hard on that hot button. But then she surprised me. I guess she'd really appreciated the rim job I'd given her earlier, because she cradled my asscheeks and lifted my butt up off the mattress. She began to lick and fuck my asshole with her tongue, and I was the one to lose my words now. I couldn't believe how good she rimmed me. It was like she was trying to make me climax without any pressure to my clit. I thought she might actually succeed, the way she alternated in her pressure, fucking my asshole hard with her tongue, and then backing off and teasing me with only the tip. As I teetered on the brink of what I could tell would be an earth-shaking orgasm, she switched things up once more. Mackenzie returned to eating my pussy, but she used my own copious juices on her fingertips and impaled my ass with her pointer and middle finger. She finger-fucked my asshole while sealing her mouth to my pussy, and I came in waves that seemed unending. She didn't stop until I physically pushed her away from my body, unable to take any more pleasure, not even a flicker. I was completely demolished, flat out on the mattress, feeling as if she'd liquefied me with bliss.

Mackenzie stood and pulled off her dress. Then she peeled off the boots and her undergarments. The scarf had fallen off during our fucking, and her makeup was smeared beyond saving. In a heartbeat, she was Mack again. Mack with a little glitter and cherry-colored lipstick. Mack who wrapped me in his strong arms and said, "I don't need a strap-on for what I'm going to do to you now."

As Mack lifted the bottle of lube from the nightstand, I rolled over and pressed my face into the pillow. He'd prepped me good with that rim job. Now I felt the glistening oil slickening me up even further. He'd gotten hard again by eating me out. His rock-like cock pressed against my hole, and then gently pushed through the tightness. I muffled my cries in the pillow as he fucked my ass as hard and fast as I'd fucked his.

"You're going to come from me fucking your asshole," Mack

said, and I nodded. He was right. "Touch your clit while I fuck you. Let yourself go."

I obeyed his command, images flickering through my head as he worked me. I thought of how sexy Mack can be when he dresses as a girl, and how sexy he can be when he's 100 percent my guy.

I love how we play—me on top, him on top, a power exchange that is unending and circular. When I came, I cried out his name. Mack responded by filling my ass with his cream and then collapsing on top of me. I looked around the room in a daze, seeing his teal dress dangling from the back of the chair. Some people say clothes make the man, but Mack and I know the flip side can be true, as well.

An Annual Affair

Natalie Perkins

I first met Aaron two years ago at an art festival in Arizona, where we were juried exhibitors. Aaron came from Denver to present his handmade glass creations, while I was in from San Diego to sell my boutique bath soaps and lotions. Aaron came around the canvas wall separating our exhibit spaces and introduced himself. "I'm going to find something to eat," he said. "Can I get you something, too?"

He was slim but broad-shouldered, with riveting blue eyes, unruly dark hair, and a strong jaw. He had an intriguing smile, too—sincere and a little intense. My heart skipped a beat.

"Sure, that'd be great," I said, brushing a lock of my blonde hair out of my eyes. I could see him sizing me up, as I had done him. His gaze took in the swell of my firm, round breasts and the slender curve of my hips. A small smile played at his lips.

"Okay. Back in a flash." He headed off down the street toward the food vendors. A few minutes later he returned with two plates of barbecued shish kebabs. We sat on chairs behind our tents and ate together. Aaron wasn't big on small talk, but that only made him more appealing. When I asked about his lovely work—vases, jewelry, and colorful baubles of all sorts—he warmed to his topic and spoke effusively about the art of glassblowing. Beneath all the shoptalk, waves of sexual attraction swirled between us. I saw in Aaron's eyes the same desire that he saw in mine. When you feel something mutual like that, something so powerful and electrifying that you can't concentrate on anything else, you know you have to act on it. I wanted to slip away with Aaron and find someplace where we could indulge our passions.

At five o'clock, the art show's first day concluded. My new friend and I went to dinner together. After that, we went to my hotel room. Sex with Aaron was deliciously intense, but it was also pure fun. He had a hefty cock, and he knew how to use it. He stayed the night with me, and the night after that, too.

When the festival wrapped up Sunday afternoon, we finally said good-bye. That could have been the end of it, but it wasn't. We kept in touch long-distance. At last year's festival, we picked up where we'd left off, going so far as to book a single hotel room to share. The arrangement was perfect. We sold our wares by day and fucked for hours on the big hotel bed each night until we were completely, wonderfully exhausted.

Naturally, we arranged to be together again at this year's event. And this time I brought a surprise for Aaron, something to add a little spice to our erotic exploits. When we arrived at our exhibitor tents the first morning, I gave him the present. He tore off the gift wrap and held up the bottle. "Organic body oil," he said, reading the label. "New product?"

I nodded. "It's a tester. If you like it, I'll add it to the product line."

He turned the bottle around and read: *"Effective as both a massage oil and personal lubricant."* Aaron grinned widely, and I saw a mischievous twinkle in his eyes. "This is absolutely perfect. Especially because—well, look." He pulled a small wooden box from his packing crates. "I made this for you. Open it."

Inside the velvet-lined enclosure was the most beautiful glass dildo I had ever seen. Ribbons of orange and gold twisted together along the inside, while beads of cobalt blue radiated outward toward the clear, smooth surface.

"It's handblown," Aaron said softly. "One of a kind. That's borosilicate glass—extremely hard and very safe."

I took the dildo out of the box and held it in my hands. As I recovered from the shock of its striking visual appeal, I studied its contours with new understanding. It was a toy ideally suited for anal play—a bit large, perhaps, but not dauntingly so, with a flared base and a tapered crown for easy rear entry. I felt a liquefying jolt of excitement between my legs. Aaron and I had done many things during our previous encounters, but we had never had anal sex. Suddenly that seemed like an inexcusable oversight!

I met Aaron's salacious grin with one of my own. "It's beautiful," I said, feeling the heat spread across my face. Aaron was going to probe my ass with his exquisite glass dildo that very evening. First, he would make its seamless surface slick with a generous coating of my new lube, and then he'd push that colorful phallus between my asscheeks and fuck me with it. And after that, after the toy had plundered my rear depths to our mutual satisfaction, I would take his flesh-and-blood cock there, and make him pound me hard until we both came.

Aaron was watching me closely. He seemed to know exactly what I was thinking. I fondled the toy a moment longer before putting it back in its box. "Thank you," I whispered, kissing him. "I can't wait to try it out."

He chuckled. "If you like it, I'll make more. No two are exactly the same."

"I already like it," I said. "Can we leave now?"

He was pleased, and more than a little excited himself. "Patience," he said. "We just got here."

But patience has never been my strong suit. For the rest of the day, Aaron's lovely creation called to me. I was so eager to feel it inside myself that I hatched a desperate plan. When Aaron went off in the afternoon to get us a snack, I hurried over to his area, found the lube, and hastened back to my side. No customers were present, so I went behind my tent with the toy and quickly greased it up. My hands trembled as I reached under my skirt and pulled my panties aside. It took only a minute to work the whole toy into my bottom. Sparks of intense pleasure stole my breath away. I straightened up, smoothed my skirt, and took a deep breath, feeling my rear passage acclimate itself to its new friend.

"Natalie?"

I stepped back into my tent and found Aaron bearing slices of pizza on paper plates. I tried to act normal, but with the toy seated snugly inside my ass, it was almost impossible. I had a naughty secret, and I felt incredibly turned on. I moved rather gingerly for the remaining hour of the art festival, thrilled by the sensual fullness and the exquisite weight pressing against my back door from the inside. We went directly from the festival to a restaurant for dinner, where I discovered that sitting on a firm chair produced a whole new surge of sensations in my derriere. I couldn't resist squirming, which rocked the toy within my depths.

"Okay, what's up with you?" Aaron asked. "You've been fidgety for hours."

"It's the dildo," I whispered. "It's inside my ass right now."

He broke into a grin. "You are bad, you know that?"

"Mm-hmm," I said, nodding and grinning sheepishly.

To say we ate fast would be an understatement. Back at our hotel room, we headed straight for the bed. I got Aaron's pants down and traced my fingers over the outline of his cock, which loomed large in his boxer briefs. Before I could free it, however, Aaron rolled me onto my stomach and flipped my skirt up. "Your panties are soaked," he said, touching me there. "What's got you so aroused, bad girl?"

"You know." I raised my hips and waggled my ass at him.

Pulling aside my panties, he took hold of the base of the toy where it emerged from my bottom. "You mean this?" He tugged on it, without pulling it out.

I closed my eyes and saw pre-orgasmic fireworks. "Yes," I rasped, nearly overcome with blissful sensations. "Oh yes, do it again."

Aaron hooked his fingers around the flared base and tugged and pushed repeatedly, making me squirm with unbearable delight. With his other hand he stroked and kneaded the globes of my ass. "You are so naughty," he said. "You took your new toy and plugged your backside hours ago."

"I couldn't resist." I heard a whimper escape my lips. "Don't make me wait, Aaron."

"Wait for what?" he demanded. "What do you want me to do with this, Natalie?"

"I want you to fuck me with it," I said, my voice stronger now. "Fuck my ass with that beautiful glass dick. Then slide your own cock in there."

He pulled the toy out all the way. Immediately I longed to have it back. Thankfully Aaron reinserted it at once. He began pumping it in and out, fucking my ass the way I wanted. The friction felt so good that I began to moan. I reached back and dipped my fingers into my pussy, then rubbed the wetness over my clit. "Oh fuck!" I groaned. "That's it, keep shoving it in there." A sudden climax swept over me, robbing me of my senses. I shook uncontrollably in the throes of primal pleasure. Aaron had just the right touch. He knew exactly when to cram the dildo in deep, when to hold it there and wiggle it, and when, finally, to ease it out.

Eventually, my violent trembling subsided and my head cleared. I lay for a moment on the sweat-soaked sheets, regaining control of my breath. My passion was nowhere near vanquished, however. Aaron put the toy aside and stripped off his briefs. When he turned back to me on the bed, his giant prick bobbed enticingly with a drop of precome leaking from the tip. I sat up and licked the salty fluid from the bulbous crown. It was a much rounder, fatter crest than the dildo featured—in fact his whole cock was bigger, in every way. I found myself wondering for the first time whether I'd really be able to accommodate such a brawny dick in my ass. I was eager to try.

"Where's the lube?" Aaron asked. His voice was husky with

need. My purse was on the floor by the bed; I leaned over, grabbed the bottle, and squeezed a copious amount of the silky liquid into my cupped hand. As I applied it to Aaron's cock, I could feel the thick shaft pulse and throb in my grasp. My arousal flared anew as I whirled around on all fours and presented my tush to Aaron. "I've been wanting this all day," I said, looking back at him.

"Me, too. You have no idea." He massaged some lube into my tiny hole. I felt the first nudge of his glans against my anus, and then seconds later it pushed through. My eyes widened, and for a moment I couldn't assimilate the complex sensations. There was a fleeting hint of pain, quickly replaced by shock waves of inexpressible pleasure. A rush of exhilaration jolted through me. Aaron pushed forward, driving more of his stout cock into my tight passage. It felt similar to the way the toy had felt in there, only more so—the weight and the fullness and a sense of expansion, magnified by a power of ten. I rocked backward at him, making sure to take the whole length of his penis fully inside my ass. We held still for a moment, and then Aaron began to fuck me. It felt so good that tears of joy sprang to my eyes. I reached back and grabbed my ass, pulling the cheeks apart. I could feel the tight ring of muscles relaxing, welcoming Aaron's bulky intruder. He gripped my hips and thrust into me with assurance. Each time he bottomed out, filling me up back there, was a moment of pure bliss. I felt wicked and depraved and absolutely wonderful.

"That's it, Aaron," I rasped. "Keep going, fuck my ass."

He seesawed faster on his knees, plunging his manhood in and out of my back hole. His ball sac slapped against my pussy with every thrust. I lowered my head and shoulders to the mattress and begged him to do me harder as I fingered my clit. With my ass high in the air like that, Aaron's incursions were even deeper and more intense. He leaned over me and jackhammered his cock freely into my hole. "Yes, yes!" I cried out, finally overwhelmed. Sobbing into the sheets, I came with startling force. Aaron held on to my hips firmly, pitched forward one final time, and uncorked his load. I could feel every spurt, every throb of his cock deep inside me. The gooey wetness filled my inner channel and triggered orgasmic aftershocks that wracked my body.

We were pretty wiped out after that. Aaron rolled off me, and I fell asleep with my head on his shoulder, deeply contented. We slept late and barely made it to the art festival in time for the next day's opening. The morning went well, though, and the afternoon did, too. Aaron and I both moved a lot of product, but to be honest, sales were not foremost on my mind. Instead, our amazing bout of anal sex occupied my thoughts all day. It had been quite a workout, and I wanted more. I had no doubt that Aaron did, too. Together we'd opened up a whole new avenue to explore, and I was anxious to continue the journey as soon as possible. Just thinking about it sent a twinge through my cunt and got my juices flowing. By the time we packed up in the afternoon, I was practically beside myself with impatience.

This time we went straight to the hotel; dinner could wait. "I want to give you a full-body massage," I said as Aaron drove. "Plenty of oil left." He glanced at me, and I saw him take in the magnitude of my lust. He knew I had much more than a mere massage in mind.

Once in our room, I ordered Aaron to strip and lie on the bed. Without a word, he got out of his clothes and lay down on his stomach. *Perfect*, I thought to myself, eyeing the muscular globes of his ass. I found the bottle of oil where we'd left it in the nightstand drawer. Kneeling over Aaron, I worked first on his shoulders and arms, and then moved down his back, spreading a nice sheen all over his skin. When I reached the top of his ass I traced my fingers quickly over those firm cheeks, saving them for later. As I proceeded down his legs, I could feel Aaron relaxing.

At last I returned to his glutes. Aaron was like putty in my hands—although, if he were to turn over, I was sure I'd find that his cock was firming up fast. Pouring out more oil, I rubbed the slippery stuff into his asscrack. Aaron twitched a little as my fingers moved inexorably toward his private hole. I dribbled more liquid directly on his puckered orifice, and then gently massaged it with the pad of my thumb. When I felt he was ready, I pushed my thumb inside. Aaron moaned, and I felt his anal aperture loosening, welcoming my digit. I pushed farther until my whole thumb was in there, all the way to the knuckle. Aaron groaned and lifted his ass slightly off the bed. I slid my thumb out, lubed up my index and middle fingers, and slipped those in together. Aaron loved it. He was moaning with deep-rooted pleasure and lifting his hips up to me.

I might have continued finger-fucking his ass for quite a while, but my need to get at his cock would not be delayed any longer. "Turn onto your back," I commanded. He did, exposing his raging hard-on. I stared at that marvelous erection and thought about how it was going to feel inside my bottom, but I avoided touching it for the moment. Instead, I rubbed oil all over his chest and belly and legs, letting my breasts rub against his skin as I worked. Only then did I zone in on Aaron's cock, which lay ramrod stiff against his stomach. I took it in my hands, and I gave it a coat of slick, shiny lube from stem to stern. By the time I was finished, Aaron was beyond desperate. All that rubbing of his sensitive organ, not to mention the anal foreplay, had made him absolutely mad with desire. I could hardly contain my own enthusiasm as I climbed over him and aimed his greased pole at my anal cleft. It fit snugly back there, the beefy shaft splitting my plump cheeks wide. Aaron watched me with burning eyes as I centered my rear hole atop his crown and eased downward. There was a moment's resistance, and then the swollen head pushed through and into my ass.

"God, that's tight," Aaron muttered hoarsely.

Down, down, down I sank on his rod, feeling every inch burrow deep into my tight channel. The feeling was beyond compare. The muscles in my thighs and belly clenched; my nipples tingled. When the globes of my ass mashed against Aaron's balls and I couldn't descend any farther, I let out the breath I'd been holding unconsciously. I was packed back there, completely filled up. Aaron saw how I reveled in the feelings coursing through me. He reached out and stroked my face, then moved his hands lower to caress my breasts.

I rocked my hips forward, and then rolled them back, sitting in Aaron's lap with his monster prick buried in my fanny. The motion tweaked my clutching anus in a way that sent shivers of delight all through my body. Aaron began to flex his hips beneath me, doubling the sensations. His hands smothered my breasts and his fingers lightly pinched my nipples, making me tremble. I closed my eyes and began to ride up and down on his pole. It felt gargantuan inside me, especially on each descent, when I crammed every last millimeter into my backside.

The fat head of his cock, meanwhile, was so far up my rear channel that I experienced waves of bliss I'd never known before. I went crazy, jacking my body up and down on Aaron's staff with all the strength I had. The bed frame groaned; the headboard rattled. Lying under me, Aaron squeezed my breasts and stroked my sides, loving every minute. I felt complete with his cock boring inside me that way, pervading my whole being. I pressed a hand to my cunt to toy with my clit and felt my juices flowing copiously. I wanted it to last longer but only managed to thrash atop Aaron's prick for a few minutes more before I came. The intensity was too much, the exquisite sense of fullness too impossibly good. I felt my insides clench up; my asshole flexed around the meaty intruder. I heard myself shout. Sitting down hard on Aaron's dick, I grabbed his shoulders and quaked through the rest of my climax. It went on for some time, but before the end, my pulsating back door coaxed forth Aaron's cream. He held my thighs, looked deep into my eyes, and went rigid all over. An instant later I felt the warm gush I'd been waiting for as his penis erupted in my ass. When the powerful throbs finally abated and Aaron was spent, I collapsed beside him on the bed.

When the weekend was over, saying good-bye to Aaron was harder than ever. But we each had a new product line to pursue back home—and red-hot memories to keep us excited about the next time we'd be able to meet.

Mistress's Surprise

SANDY BAXTER

I had known for some time that one of my husband's favorite fantasies involved him being fucked in the ass with a strap-on dildo. Eric was quick to point out that it wasn't something he wanted to do all the time, but he'd been dreaming about it for years and wanted to experience it firsthand, to see if real life was as good as his imagination. His desire was so strong that he even went out and bought a strap-on harness and a lifelike black dildo to go with it. However, despite his eagerly made purchase, we hadn't yet taken the plunge. I found the idea somewhat appealing, but I'm not usually the dominant type, so the notion got pushed to the back of my mind. To be honest, it was also probably because I was a little bit nervous. I wasn't sure about taking the lead and topping my husband in that way, even though I knew it was something he wanted. I have to admit that when I was digging around in my closet and came across our bag of sex toys, I felt some guilt that I hadn't been more proactive about fulfilling Eric's fantasy. I knew that bag held a harness and dildo that had never even been taken out of their packages because of my own reluctance to be the dominant partner my lover craved—if only for one night.

That was when I made up my mind to be for him what he has been for me: a lover willing to try anything in order to give the other partner satisfaction. So I sat down and dreamt up a plan to make it right. First, I took the harness and the dildo out of the packages and really looked at them. The harness was made of a leather-like material and had straps that went around each leg and the waist. I was glad it was not the thong-panty kind because those always looked uncomfortable to wear. I decided to try it on, so I pulled off my jeans and pulled the harness up over my panties. Once I fiddled around with the straps a bit, I got it seated properly on my hips. The dildo was supposed to attach to a ring that was held in place by four heavy-duty straps and snaps. I was surprised by how authentic the silicone cock was shaped, with the texture of the veins and the mushroom-shaped cap at the end—just like a real penis. In overall size, it was smaller than Eric's fully erect cock, but I guessed that he was nervous about taking a big dick up his ass. We had fooled around with anal play many times in the past, but it was always merely a finger or a tiny butt plug. He'd never had a toy of this size inside his asshole.

I unfastened two of the snaps that held the ring in place, and then inserted the dildo through the metal circle and reattached the snaps. Looking down at the cock sticking out between my legs shocked me at first. Men are used to looking down there and seeing their dicks, but this was all new to me—and it was turning me on. I couldn't resist giving my hips a little shake that made the toy bob up and down. Looking in the full-length mirror offered an even more dramatic sight, and I couldn't believe I had waited so long to try this toy on for size.

I decided it would be really cool if I wore the dildo and harness underneath my clothing, and then surprised Eric while we were out for dinner. Slipping on one of my short, tight skirts, I immediately saw the flaw in that plan. The dildo bulged underneath the garment in such a way that it looked like I had quite a nice package. Plan B involved me wearing a full peasant skirt, and when I pulled the harness up in the back and down in the front, the dildo was positioned between my legs and couldn't be detected. I sat down to test my plan, and other than the strange feeling of having a silicone dildo rubbing against my bare thighs, it worked quite well. I pulled out a sexy black corset that had been worn very few times and tried it on. It barely contained my boobs, but if I wore my loose-fitting embroidered blouse over it, no one would know what was underneath. If I added some thigh-high black stockings, the outfit would be complete. Once Eric saw me without the blouse and skirt, I was certain that the sight of me would make him as horny as hell.

A week later, Eric and I were out at one of our favorite restaurants enjoying glasses of wine in our usual corner booth, and I was ready to spring the trap.

"Honey," I cooed as I slid closer to him on the banquette seat, "I have a surprise for you that I think you'll enjoy."

Before Eric could respond, the waiter approached and asked if we were ready to order.

"Not quite yet," I replied. "Give us a few minutes."

"A surprise?" Eric asked after the waiter had departed.

I took Eric's hand and placed it on my thigh. Then I pulled my skirt up almost to my waist, confident that no one could see past the voluminous white table linens. I moved Eric's hand to my silicone cock and looked him right in the eye so I could see his expression.

"Is that—" Eric's eyes were almost bulging with shock.

"Yep, it sure is," I said with pride.

The waiter was heading over again, so I waved him off with my free hand, but he must have thought Eric looked a bit strange. If he had only known what I had nestled between my legs.

"We are going home right after dinner. No dessert. And when we get there, you're going to strip naked, and I'm going to put a butt plug up your ass. Then I have more surprises for you, but at some point I plan to ram my dick up your ass and fuck the daylights out of you."

The waiter headed back to our table, and I ordered for us since Eric seemed to be incapable of speaking. To say we made fast work of our dinners would be an understatement. It was more like a speed-eating contest with a call for the check before we'd even finished our entrees.

Once we were back at the house, I willed myself to take total charge, even though being dominant does not come naturally to me. Eric headed for the bedroom, but I pulled him back by the arm.

"No," I said firmly. "The kitchen." Eric followed me as I instructed.

"Take off all your clothes," I directed.

"But—" I put my hand over Eric's mouth to silence him.

"I'm in charge now. You'll do what I say, and you'll do it without question. In fact, I don't even want you to speak unless I ask you to. Understood?"

Eric nodded his assent. This role reversal, with me being so dominant, was clearly exciting him. That was even more apparent when he stripped off his clothes and I could see his enormous erection.

"Bend over and grab your ankles," I commanded.

Eric did as he was told, and I retrieved the butt plug and lubricant from where I had stashed them in a kitchen cabinet. I put plenty of lube on the plug and then more on Eric's asshole. When I pushed a finger partially into his tight passage, his body went rigid but he maintained his position. The fact that he was trying so hard to obey me made my pussy tingle. I was starting to like being in charge. I could only imagine how exciting the rest of the night would be. Taking a deep breath to steady myself, I then inserted the butt plug into Eric's ass and eased it forward and then back, but each stroke went farther in than the last. Eric's breathing got more erratic as I worked his back door, but he was starting to tense up.

"Relax," I told him sternly, more as a command than advice. There was no way I was going to be able to fuck him if he stayed worked up the way he was. Eric understood and relaxed his muscles. I could tell that he was still on edge, but he stopped clenching his asscheeks, easing the passage of the slippery toy.

I pressed forward insistently, unceasingly, and then finally forced the plug up past the widest portion and watched his asshole close around the neck of the toy. I was satisfied that it would stay in place and work its magic.

"You may stand up now—and put your hands behind your back," I told him.

Once he was standing, I grabbed some cuffs and bound his wrists together behind his back.

"Follow me to the living room now."

Once there, I tossed a pillow on the floor near the sofa. "Kneel," I demanded, pointing down at the cushion.

Eric got down on his knees carefully, as he did not have the use of his arms for balance. I stayed close by in case he needed any assistance, but he managed to make it all on his own.

I began to remove my blouse, and as I did so, Eric hungrily eyed my every move. My breasts were almost bursting out the top of my corset and certainly got his attention. Then I unfastened my skirt and let it drop to the floor. Eric's gaze instantly dropped to the black cock. There was a look of excitement mixed with fear on his face. I moved closer and stood before him so that my dick was directly in front of his lips.

"I want you to lick my dick."

"But—" he started to say in protest.

My reaction was swift. I slapped Eric's face hard. Not hard enough to make his ears ring, but hard enough to sting and make his cheek red. His look of shock was something I had never seen before, and I felt a twinge of excitement in my cunt. I was quickly realizing that a dominant woman had been lurking deep inside me all along. It was a deliciously wicked discovery.

"You're not in control tonight—I am. So you do as I command or I will punish your ass in a way you won't forget. Nod if that's understood."

Eric nodded. I could tell that he was shocked but pleased with how the evening was progressing.

"Now, let's try this again. I want you to lick my dick and keep licking it until I tell you to stop."

I placed the black cock against his lips, and Eric started

running his tongue up and down the shaft. I held the toy steady so he could access all sides of it, and soon it was glistening with his saliva. Then I began to rub the toy against his face, spreading the saliva on his chin, cheeks, and nose before pulling back to keep the toy just out of his reach.

"Keep going," I hissed, and Eric tried in vain to get his tongue back on my dick. I laughed at his struggle and watched his face grow redder with frustration and embarrassment.

"Well, if you can't lick any better than that, let's see how well you can suck. Open your mouth."

Eric hesitated briefly, but he must have still felt the sting of my slap. He parted his lips, and I pushed the cock forward harshly, which made him gag.

"You'll learn quickly, my little cocksucker. When we're done tonight, you'll be a pro."

Eric's eyes grew wide, but I could sense his excitement. His fantasy wasn't going according to his original plan, but each of us was clearly turned on by this course of events.

I eased the cock back and forth between his lips, fascinated by how much of the dick he was able to swallow. I made him take the toy deeper with each thrust of my hips, fucking his mouth as he had done to mine many times. Finally, I pulled the shaft out and ran the tip around his lips one more time. He stayed still, letting me play my game, and his obedience thrilled me. Sensing his total submission, I pulled back and unfastened his wrists.

"On your back—now."

Once Eric had obeyed, I knelt over his face and got in a sixty-nine position so that I could insert my dick back into his mouth while

I took his cock in my hands. Instead of giving him the blow job he might have been expecting, I began to give him a very sensual hand job. Whenever I could tell that he was getting extremely excited, I released his shaft and sensed his disappointment. I continued to tease him this way—stroking him and choking back his climax at the last minute—while I made him continue to suck my dick. After making Eric crazy with arousal, I decided it was time for him to get his wish.

"Get up and bend over the arm of the sofa," I ordered.

Eric may have been relieved that the cocksucking and tortuous hand job were over, but now he had to face the reality of being fucked in the ass. I pulled the butt plug out very slowly and hoped that it had done its job of stretching his opening in preparation for my dildo. I put a healthy coat of lubricant on the silicone and got in position behind Eric, who was holding himself perfectly still as he awaited my next move. I inserted just the head of the slippery cock into his asshole and watched his body tense up. His muscles were clinging tightly to the head of the fake dick, and it seemed as if he was holding his breath. I pulled the toy completely out and then pushed only the tip of it back in. I did this over and over, slowly and rhythmically, to help him relax. Then I left the tip of the cock in his ass and began to gradually inch forward. Eric was moaning softly, his whispered utterances betraying his arousal. After a while, I picked up the pace and shoved the cock deeper in his back hole. Soon, his buttcheeks lifted higher each time I rammed the toy home, and I was lost in the hypnotic motion of the slick black dick gliding in and out of Eric's beautiful butt.

But then I remembered that I wanted Eric to experience some other positions, so I extracted the dildo.

"We're not finished," I said in a matter-of-fact tone. "Now I want you on your back on the ottoman."

Eric got off the sofa, and then he lay down on the big, over-sized, tufted-leather ottoman. His eyes avoided mine, and his cheeks were flushed red.

"Pull your knees up to your chest."

I got into position between his legs and reinserted the dildo into his asshole. With Eric holding his legs up, I was able to get greater leverage as I moved the cock in and out like a piston. Eric had used the position with me when he wanted to get his cock deep inside my pussy. Now, turnabout was fair play as I drove the cock deep into his clutching hole. My thighs slapped against his as I kept up the pace, and I was sweating from the exertion, all the while feeling my pussy dripping like a faucet.

"This is too much effort," I gasped after a few minutes, pulling away from him. "It's time for you to do some work, too. Stand up."

Once Eric was upright, I switched positions so that I was on my back.

"I want you to crouch over me and lower yourself onto my dick. You're going to fuck yourself silly."

Getting into position as instructed, Eric hovered above the dildo and then slowly lowered his ass onto it.

"Take it all the way in," I commanded, seeing a host of emotions flash over his face as he obeyed me: lust, embarrassment, passion. "I want you to feel it all the way up to the hilt. Balls-deep. And then I want you to slide your ass up and down. If you get it right, I'll make you come like a rocket."

As Eric followed my instructions and shamelessly took his

pleasure from the toy strapped to my pelvis, I began massaging his cock and balls. My husband's movements made the base of the dildo press against the top of my slit, and the pressure teased my lust-swollen clit. My arousal spiraled upward as he rode my cock with wild abandon. The more energetic his movement became, the more I pumped his shaft, and in just a few minutes I surrendered to orgasm. Seconds later, Eric groaned and his load was spurting all over my breasts. When our orgasms subsided, I opened my arms and he slouched forward with his face next to mine. I showered his neck with tender little kisses and felt his body relax and melt into my embrace.

"Was that everything you'd dreamed it could be?"

"Mmm," was all Eric said in reply.

"Well, I have news for you. This won't be the last time. There are so many toys out there that I want to use on you, and you're going to love them—trust me."

"Whatever you say, Mistress," he uttered in an awed whisper.

At that moment I knew I was going to have a lot of fun unlocking all of my husband's secret fantasies—and looked forward to enacting some of mine.

South of the Border

BRAD WARNER

The flight from San Francisco to Cancun wasn't full, which surprised me. Then again, not everyone was trying to recover from the kind of grueling work schedule I had just completed—a month of double shifts, all-nighters, and enough tension to last a lifetime. But the company had met its goal, and as a reward to myself, I was flying to Mexico's Mayan Riviera for a vacation.

I had a window seat. The two seats next to me were still vacant about five minutes before the plane pushed back from the gate, so I figured I'd stretch out and catch some Zs. It didn't work out that way. Just before they sealed the door, one more person boarded. She was a pretty brunette with green eyes, a delicate nose, and a sensual mouth—plus a figure that turned every head as she made her way down the aisle. I couldn't believe my luck when she stopped at my row and dropped into the middle seat, right next to me. Wearing shorts, a fitted T-shirt, and sandals, she was already dressed for Cancun. From the corner of my eye, I admired the lush swell of her breasts and her long, shapely legs. She had a dynamite ass, too, but I wouldn't discover that until later.

She buckled up and then turned to me with a cute smile. "Hi, I'm Drew."

"Hey, Drew, nice to meet you," I said. "I'm Brad."

"First time to Cancun?" she asked.

"Yep. I can hardly wait. How about you?"

She nodded. "Me, too. I need to feel the sun on my skin and sand between my toes." Sinking back into her seat, she closed her eyes for a moment. "Give me a tropical beach, a bikini, and a drink with a little umbrella in it, and I'm happy."

I blinked, looking at her, and of course the image flew into my mind, too. I don't know how closely my picture lined up with Drew's, but in mine, she wore the smallest swimsuit imaginable, and her golden skin was aglow with suntan oil.

Drew and I continued talking throughout takeoff and all the way up to cruising altitude. She and I were about the same age—I'm twenty-seven—and we totally clicked. You can really get to know a person when you're thrown together on a long flight like that. Drew could've moved to the aisle seat for more room, but she didn't seem to mind being crammed in next to me, our shoulders and knees touching. I didn't mind, either—far from it. She smelled great, like a fresh spring breeze, and she proved to be as smart and funny as she was attractive. Most exciting of all was the strength of the sexual chemistry blooming between us. It was so intoxicating that I felt like I'd had a few margaritas already. Once it came out that we were both single, the sparks *really* started flying. Drew shared some of her innermost thoughts and made it pretty clear that she was an uninhibited, sexually adventurous person. I would have had to be blind to miss the signals she was sending me. I wanted her just as badly, but then the plane began its descent into Cancun, and I realized we might only have a few more minutes together.

The same thought was bothering Drew. "Maybe we could share a taxi," she blurted out.

That seemed unlikely, but I asked where she was staying. When she told me, I had a sudden sensation of weightlessness, as if the plane had abruptly lost altitude. In reality, though, our flight was perfectly smooth.

"You're kidding," I finally managed to say.

She stared at me with wide emerald eyes. "What's the matter?"

There must be hundreds, maybe thousands of places to stay in and around the greater Cancun resort area. However improbable it may seem—and believe me, I've thought about this often since then—Drew and I were both booked at the same resort. It was an incredible coincidence, an unbelievable stroke of luck. When I explained the situation, Drew felt certain I was putting her on. I dug around in my bag for my reservation and showed it to her. She broke into such a bright, sexy smile that I knew my whole vacation outlook had just improved tenfold.

"So we *are* going to share a taxi," she said, right before giving me a long, passionate kiss. It was so good I missed the entire landing.

After going through customs and immigration, Drew and I exited the airport and walked out to the curb to hail a cab. She was a pace or two ahead of me, and that's when I got my first good look at her backside. She had the most fantastic butt, full and round yet perfectly proportioned with the rest of her fit body.

The air was so warm and moist, and the light of the setting sun so ethereal, that it felt like we had arrived on a different planet. I put my window down in the cab and off we went. Toward the end of the ride Drew dozed with her head on my shoulder. I should have been tired, too, but as I looked down at Drew's dark, wavy hair and her pretty face in repose against my chest, I felt completely alive.

She woke up when our taxi stopped in front of the hotel's elaborate entrance. A short while later I tagged along as the porter led Drew to her accommodations. She had a first-floor suite that looked out on beautiful manicured grounds and, beyond, the sparkling ocean. I gave her a kiss and turned to follow the porter to my own room. Drew grabbed my arm and whispered, "Don't be long."

I wasn't. I merely dropped off my bags, changed into shorts and a fresh shirt, and splashed some water on my face. On my way out I grabbed the complimentary bottle of champagne that had been left on ice for me.

Drew opened her door at my knock and welcomed me in. The room was dusky, the sun having set a few minutes earlier. She had opened the sliding glass door facing the beach, but not the gauzy white curtain, which swelled in the breeze. Sounds of music and laughter from the pool area wafted into the room.

I turned to face Drew. She wore a hotel bathrobe and nothing else. The sash was untied, revealing the inside curves of her breasts, her flat belly and, farther down, the intriguing *V* of her crotch. I saw that she was completely shaved.

"We won't be needing that," she said, nodding at the bottle of champagne in my hand. I glanced around. Of course—she had her own bottle on ice, a welcome gift from the resort.

"Well, then," I said, "what *do* you need?"

She stepped close and playfully grabbed the bulge in my shorts. "This."

Obviously, the time for subtlety was over. I put the champagne down and gathered her in my embrace a trifle more roughly than I'd intended. Drew melted into me, her body warm and yielding. She had taken a shower; her hair and skin were still damp. She smelled better than ever, her scent something tropical and flowery. When we kissed, her lips were full and soft, her tongue eager.

"It's much too warm and humid in here for this, don't you think?" I said, pushing the robe off Drew's shoulders. She stepped back and let the robe drop to the floor, exposing herself completely to my hungry eyes. I slipped my hands around her waist to her ass and squeezed those supple, firm cheeks. She pulled desperately at my shirt, so I took over and lifted it over my head. She transferred her attention to my shorts. In a minute I was nude, too. We stumbled to the big four-poster canopy bed and collapsed onto it, our movements hasty with pent-up lust. My hand found the smooth lips of her sex, and I dipped a finger into her wetness and probed her folds. Drew moaned and spread her thighs wide, opening her cunt to deeper exploration. I found her clit and rolled that swelling button beneath my thumb until Drew sighed with pleasure.

"Let me see your cock," she soon demanded, a slave to her desire. Sitting up, she took her measure of my manhood, which lay stiff against my belly. She stroked it lovingly, her eyes bright in the twilight.

Then she dropped her head and took me into her mouth, sucking ardently. I watched as she bobbed, enjoying both the sight and feel of her lips on my penis. When she came up for air she kept her hand on my wet shaft and said, "I love how thick and long you are. You're going to feel so good in my bum."

Her use of the British term was the first thing that got my attention, but then the full import of what she'd said burst upon me. The mere thought of fucking this gorgeous woman in the ass made my hard-on grow an extra inch. I love anal sex, and Drew, I discovered, absolutely *craved* it, which proved once more that we were perfectly matched. She was already positioning herself on top of me, trembling with anticipation. Once seated astride my hips, she took hold of my dick and rubbed its crown in the juicy folds of her sex. Little gasps of pleasure escaped her lips. With her free hand she grabbed a bottle of lube that she'd placed on the nightstand and proceeded to grease me up.

I reached out and caressed Drew's fine breasts while awaiting the feel of her warm, clenching anus around my cockhead. When it came, it was even better than I'd anticipated. Drew held my rod straight up, aiming at her tiny hole, and then slowly lowered herself. Her sphincter resisted my bulbous glans for a brief moment and then relented. Inch by inch, the rest of my thick shaft disappeared into Drew's tight back channel. She took her time, moaning with delight all the while, until she had my entire length buried inside her back door. "Ahh, that's it," she said, her face etched with intense pleasure. The sensations emanating all along the length of my cock were indescribable. I realized I was holding my breath and let out a long, slow exhalation of contentment. Drew was in a similar place. She squeezed her eyes shut and sat still for a moment, acclimating herself to the feeling of fullness. I felt her back hole relaxing, its grip wonderfully firm and yet accommodating, too. Then our primal urges began to reassert themselves. Drew pressed her open palms to my chest and began to flex her haunches with a grace and skill that was totally erotic. She rode my pole gently at first, but soon lapsed into the hard, all-out fucking she so desperately craved.

"Yeah, baby, go for it," I said, my words punctuated by Drew's violent up-and-down movements. I stroked her thighs and hips as she rammed my cock into her tiny hole. Her hair, tangled and matted with sweat, was flying everywhere. The fury of our coupling combined with the high humidity of our location made us both slick from head to toe.

"Oh god, yes!" she stammered, looking me in the eye through her wild tresses. "You're so deep, so fucking deep inside me." She reared up, arching her torso and squeezing her breasts in her hands. She began to power her lithe body up and down on my dick with such enthusiasm that she almost made me come at once. Somehow I held off, but I knew it wouldn't be long before I filled her ass with cream. I'd thought my dick was already stuffed inside there as far as it could go, but her new straight-up position drove me even farther up her channel. The way she ground herself down against my root was so savage—her head thrown back, her eyes slitted with passion—that I couldn't contain myself any longer. I bucked my hips off the mattress and my whole body went rigid as my seed pulsed into Drew's rear end. She was lost in a mammoth climax of her own; I could feel her palpitating ring of muscle as it clenched and released the base of my cock, coaxing every last drop of semen from my balls.

Afterward we lay in the dark, listening to the ocean and the sound of each other's breathing. In a little while Drew got up to close the sliding door and turn on the air conditioner. She came back to bed, and we were both asleep in minutes. Sometime after midnight we awoke, famished. I called room service, and Drew opened the champagne.

I seldom saw the inside of my own room after that night, and when I did it was with Drew, who insisted we give my bed as thorough a workout as we had been giving hers all week. The positions she knew for anal sex were as endless as her enthusiasm, and I'm happy to report that we tried them all.

One day toward the end of the week, Drew and I joined a tour group visiting the Mayan ruins at nearby Tulum. Our guide's chatter eventually grew wearisome, so we slipped away from the group to explore the site on our own. Dirt paths wended among the ancient structures lying half in ruin, baking in the sun. The site is perched on a cliff above a beautiful beach. Wooden stairs lead down to the teal-blue sea, where tourists often enjoy a refreshing dip. Drew and I stripped down to our bathing suits and waded out to chest-deep water. She started getting frisky, rubbing her ass against the front of my swim trunks until my cock became a big, hard bulge. We both got so horny that we went ashore, ascended the stairs to the top of the bluff again, and began looking around for someplace private.

Eventually we found ourselves on a little-used path into the jungle. We left the other tourists behind and kept walking until we spotted a crumbling stone terrace off in the brambles. This structure was small and unimpressive compared to the others back at the main site, but it would serve our purpose well. A dozen steps brought us around to the rear of the edifice, where, if we kept behind the tallest part of the wall, we would be completely out of sight of anyone passing by.

Offering me a lustful grin, Drew reached into the pocket of her skimpy white shorts and produced a bottle of lube—an item I learned early on that Drew is rarely without. She handed it to me, and then pulled off her shorts and the bikini bottom underneath. Turning toward the wall, she spread her hands on the stone surface and stood with her feet wide apart in the brush. Then she thrust her ass out toward me expectantly. For a moment I could only stare at her delectable behind, beautifully awash in golden sunlight. Stark tan lines showed the ghost of her Brazilian bikini bottom, a nice contrast to the deep golden honey color bestowed on the rest of her skin by the Yucatan sun. The succulent lips of her pussy were exposed, too, gleaming with dewy wetness. For the umpteenth time I marveled at my luck in meeting Drew. She cast me a wanton, hurry-up-and-fuck-me look over her shoulder that made my cock grow as hard as a diamond. Hastily, I dropped my trunks and applied some lube to my erection, then massaged a dollop into the cleft of Drew's butt as well. For a moment I considered sliding my dick into her cunt as a lead-in to the intense pleasures of our primary mission, but no—Drew was not in a mood to tolerate any detours, no matter how brief. Using both hands, I spread the fleshy globes of her ass, enjoying their sun-warmed plumpness. The call of a macaw rent the air as my throbbing crown entered the grip of Drew's sphincter. Pushing forward, I watched as half my rod's length vanished into her molten depths.

"Oh fuck," Drew whispered, already shoving back at me. "Each time is better than the last." Her breath came rapidly as the rest of my thick tool slid inside her back passage. Then she settled into the deep, intense sensations she was experiencing. I held on to the silky curve of her hips as she rocked forward and back on her heels, driving my cock in to the hilt. My balls smacked up against the roundness of her rump and stayed there as I held her fast against me. "Oomph," she muttered, wiggling on my cock. "Now fuck me like I know you can, Brad."

I adjusted my grip at her waist and began pumping away, driving fully into her ass. Drew's clutching orifice took the full length of my dick on each thrust, from its meaty head to its stout base. If not for the cooling wind coming off the ocean, we probably would have ended up as sweat-drenched as we'd been during our first encounter in Drew's hotel room. I liked being outside, and in that wild setting, with my cock cleaving Drew's ass, I felt like I could stay on my feet for hours. Drew, however, had other plans. Her insatiable sexual appetite eventually demanded greater intensity, and for that she wanted to fuck doggie-style.

She had just dropped to her hands and knees, with her ass jutting up high, when we heard voices. Two people were coming up the path, engrossed in conversation. I hunched low beside Drew, and we waited in silence—Drew stifling a giggle—until the couple passed. Of course, before they were completely out of earshot, Drew began waggling her fanny with impatience. Kneeling directly behind her, I brought my cock into the crack of her upraised ass and she reached back to guide me in.

"Yes, that's it," she said softly as I crammed my penis into her puckered little aperture once more. I curved my hands around her smooth tush, leaned in and gave it my all. Our doggie-style position provided deeper penetration, which was exactly what Drew wanted. She was soon clawing at the ground and reveling in ecstasy as I pummeled her derriere. Whimpering with indescribable joy, she lowered her shoulders to the ground and brought one hand back to rub at her clitoris. In a moment she devolved into a kind of primitive state, wracked by waves of elemental bliss. Somehow she kept her fingers on her clit, prolonging the orgasm while I continued sawing in and out of her clutching rear hole.

At last I felt my load well up deep within my balls. Realizing the pinnacle was at hand, I rocked hard into Drew's butt once more and felt the cream erupt from my cock. My whole body jolted involuntarily, and I grunted louder than was prudent in that public setting. Salvo after salvo of warm semen shot deep into Drew's ass. Her snug hole, so tight and yet so pliant, flexed again and again around my shaft, until my balls had given all they had to give. When I felt the last pulsating throbs die off, I pulled out of Drew's rosy bud and flopped onto the ground beside her, utterly spent and completely satisfied.

Our week in paradise ended, but Drew and I found a little more luck back home. No, she didn't live in the house next door to me, or even on the next street. But she did live in a nearby neighborhood, and we continued to see each other. In fact, Drew eventually moved in with me, giving my improbable-but-true story a fairy-tale ending.

Naughty Inspiration

Lisa Garcia

My husband makes his living as a writer, and like anyone in his profession, he can be susceptible to writer's block. Fortunately, Rudy's particular niche—he's an erotic novelist who writes under a pseudonym—makes it easy for me to help him avoid such problems. I'm his muse in a very practical sense: I help him come up with explicit scenes for his books by acting on my own salacious impulses. Rudy likes to say that my libido is "stuck in overdrive," and I guess he's right. I'm an adventurous, uninhibited woman who is absolutely crazy about sex—especially anal sex. There's a lot of backdoor action in my husband's books for the simple reason that it's my favorite kind.

Rudy knows it doesn't take much to spark my creative ideas. One Saturday last fall, for instance, he came out of his office and made a show of being frustrated. He'd been holed up all morning, working on his latest book. "I don't know, Lisa," he said, rubbing his eyes. "It's just not flowing today."

He was exaggerating; I'd heard his fingers clicking away at the computer all morning. However, that didn't mean he couldn't use a little fresh inspiration. "You need a break," I said. "Let's get out of the house. It's a beautiful day. How about a picnic?" My mind raced ahead, imagining the possibilities. "I'll put together a basket. We can have lunch in that glade behind the house. Maybe you'll get some new ideas for the book."

Rudy smiled, and I saw a twinkle in his eye. With his dark, unruly hair, mischievous blue eyes, and tall, slender frame, Rudy is as sexy-handsome today as he was when we got married five years ago. I had to fight down an impulse to take him by the hand and lead him back to the bedroom. What I had in mind would be worth the wait.

Fifteen minutes later, equipped with bread, cheese, a bottle of wine, and a blanket, we strolled along the little path that leads from our backyard into the woods. We're fortunate to live on the boundary of a large tract of national forest land. Summer was long past, but the recent spate of cold, dreary weather had given way to a glorious Indian-summer day. I wore a skimpy sundress and sandals, the better to feel the sun's rays on my skin. Rudy didn't know it yet, but I wore nothing underneath.

He glanced at my brief attire as I tripped along beside him. "I should have changed into shorts."

"I wouldn't worry about that, honey," I said coquettishly. "I imagine we'll get you out of those jeans before long."

He looked at me again, and this time his eyes lingered. He

took in my shapely legs, perky breasts and, finally, the sexy curve of my behind, which he loves most of all. I saw his hunger and felt a surge of desire well up within me. I could hardly wait to feel his cock in my ass.

Soon we arrived at the small clearing. The sun was stronger there, warming a broad patch of leaf-strewn ground. We spread out the blanket and enjoyed our modest meal in complete privacy. The picnic, though, was merely a prelude to the main event, which I was eager to get started. As soon as I finished my glass of wine, I reached back and unzipped my dress. I could feel Rudy's stare as I pulled the dress over my head, kicked off my sandals, and lay back on my elbows, completely nude. My blonde hair swirled about my shoulders in casual disarray.

"Ahh," I sighed, letting my head fall back. "This feels *so* good." And it did. After weeks of cheerless gray skies, the sunny warmth flowing all over my naked body had a kind of transportive effect. As my skin heated up, my desire rose, too. My nipples tingled and my cunt grew slick. "There's one more thing in the picnic basket, honey," I said. "Would you get it for me, please?"

Rudy reached into the basket, found the small bottle of lube and grinned. "Catch," he said, tossing it over. I snatched it out of the air. Then I opened my legs wide, exposing my naked vulva to the staring eye of the sun. I keep the whole area free of pubic hair, except for a tiny patch of blonde fleece about the size of a quarter. Reaching down between my legs, I massaged a dollop of lube into and around the rim of my anus. It felt good; I sighed with pleasure.

Finally, I looked at Rudy again. "Time to get those pants off," I said. My voice dripped with lust.

He pulled off his jeans, revealing the outline of his huge hard-on inside his boxer shorts.

"These, too," I added, sitting up and taking hold of the waist-band of his boxers.

In a moment Rudy lay half-naked beside me on the blanket. "Mmm, nice," I purred, curling my lubed hand around his big prick. I squeezed his rod and ran my fist up and down the shaft until he was thoroughly greased.

"Now lie back, and I'll give you something to write about," I declared. Rudy grinned like a Cheshire cat. When he lay prostrate I climbed atop him, aimed his meaty glans at my rear hole and impaled myself. I took the descent slow and steady, unconsciously holding my breath until the full length and width of Rudy's organ was inside my butt. It felt like every nerve in my body was focused back there, locked in on the passage of his cock through my sphincter.

No matter how often Rudy and I have anal sex, it's always a singular experience. Taking Rudy's penis in my ass is a unique and special pleasure, so intensely good as to be almost indescribable. In my world, nothing else compares.

I bottomed out in his lap, flattening his balls beneath the globes of my ass. "That's it, honey," Rudy said softly. "You've got my whole cock in there. It's so tight, so warm…" His voice drifted off as he momentarily lost himself in the sublime sensations. The fit was so snug that I could feel every pulse and every throb of his shaft inside my core. I sat back for a moment to adjust my balance and get my feet under me. Then I rolled my hips forward a bit, settling into one of my favorite positions for maximum penetration. My swollen clit pressed into Rudy's groin and sent auxiliary shivers of pleasure through my frame. I began to lift and lower myself on his pole, riding him with well-practiced vigor. He ran his hands along my flexing thighs and up the curve of my hips, then higher to my waist. He likes the feel of my whole body getting into it when I sit astride him. I arched my back and raked my fingers through my blonde hair, swept up in the sensuality of the moment.

All around us, the aspens stood watch. Their quaking leaves drifted down silently, carpeting the ground in autumn hues. Other than the chirps of a few curious birds, Rudy's grunts and my own sighs of delight were the only sounds in the clearing. My passionate cries were becoming louder and louder as I rocked atop Rudy. His hands went to my bouncing breasts and covered them, making my stiff nipples spark with pleasure. His cock felt incredibly large as it bored repeatedly into my anal channel. My sphincter began to clench and unclench around that thick probe as a climax of mammoth proportions stole upon me.

"Oh, oh—I'm coming!" My voice was strained with emotion. I pressed my hands to Rudy's chest and gyrated against him, feeling both my asshole and my cunt grind against his root. For a full minute I couldn't even see straight. My pussy juices flowed freely into Rudy's pubic hair and my anus repeatedly squeezed his cock. At last I collapsed onto Rudy's chest with his rod still inside me. I knew he was close to climaxing, too. "Keep fucking me," I whispered in his ear. "Keep fucking my ass until I feel your dick explode in there."

Rudy stroked my hair and kissed me, then rolled us both over so that he was on top. "Your ass feels incredible," he said. Deftly, he powered his prick in and out of my anal opening, his limber body rising and falling above me. My own passion stirred anew, making me writhe beneath him. Rudy rose up to his knees, and I lifted my ankles to his shoulders. He grabbed hold of my thighs and really let go, slamming his cock into my ass with lightning-quick thrusts. I reached down and toggled my clit, adding new waves of pleasure to those already flowing through me. With my other hand I reached around to squeeze one of my asscheeks and hold it apart from the other, the better to get every inch of Rudy's shaft inside me.

It took him only a few minutes longer to pass the point of no return. The semen finally erupted from his crown when it was deep in my back passage, instigating another release for me, too. I undulated against the blanket and cried out with unchecked passion. My back door massaged Rudy's penis until he gave up the last of his load. With a final shudder he pulled out and collapsed beside me. We looked up at the treetops for a while, catching our breath.

Rudy did, indeed, adapt our picnic encounter for the novel he was working on at the time, and I was only too happy to have helped. Another, more recent experience also proved useful, but this one was entirely unplanned. We were out hiking one early September day when we happened upon a stretch of two-lane blacktop that had been closed due to the construction of a four-lane expressway nearby. It was a rural area, and pretty remote, with tree-covered hills and unspoiled valleys stretching all the way to the horizon. Curious, Rudy and I stepped around the ROAD CLOSED sign and walked along the pavement for a while. We were surprised to find that it went on for about a mile, complete with yellow stripes painted down the middle. Far off in the distance, we could see where the road abruptly ended in a pile of boulders. It was a strange feeling to be able to walk freely down the middle of a perfectly good road and not worry about cars coming along. My natural inclination to view settings and situations with sexual intent soon kicked into gear.

"You know," I said to Rudy, stepping sprightly out in front of him, "this old road is completely abandoned and forgotten. We're totally alone out here. We could do anything we want."

Rudy arched an eyebrow at me. "I suppose we could," he said. "What do you have in mind?"

"Well, if there's a club for people who have fucked in the middle of a street in broad daylight, I bet it's pretty exclusive." I unzipped my shorts and dropped them to the asphalt.

"I bet you're right," he agreed.

"And you know me," I went on, removing my T-shirt and bra, "I love getting naked any old place."

"That you do," my husband remarked, smiling broadly.

I dispatched my underwear next, and stood proudly on the blacktop in nothing but my sneakers and socks. The day was mild and the light breeze felt wonderful against my bare skin. You could almost smell the change of seasons in the air as summer gave way to autumn. Caught up in a feeling of rising excitement, I threw my arms wide and danced gleefully along the yellow stripes in the middle of the road. Rudy laughed, but I could see he was getting turned on by my naked antics. The bulge in his shorts was a dead giveaway. I went back to him, and using my discarded shorts to cushion my knees, I knelt at his feet.

"You never stop," Rudy said happily.

"Mmmm," was all I could reply, because I'd extricated his hard-on from his shorts and lowered my mouth over the portly cap. Rudy's cock was warm and thick between my lips. As I swirled my tongue all over his luscious tool, I cupped his balls and rolled them in my palm. Rudy moaned and stroked my jawline with his finger. Bobbing back and forth, I sucked on his pole with such enthusiasm that, after only a minute or two, it began to twitch with the telltale signs of an impending eruption.

"Not yet," I said, sitting back on the blacktop. I wanted to save the power of his pent-up lust for my ass. I knew he did, too.

"You look good enough to eat," Rudy remarked, eyeing my curvy body and, in particular, the cleft between my legs.

"Then why don't you?" I opened my thighs wide. "Come on, taste me," I implored him.

Rudy knelt down and lowered his head to my crotch. His fingers spread my pussy lips open and his tongue snaked inside. I shuddered at the sudden delicious feeling. "Suck my clit," I pleaded, pushing my vulva against his mouth.

"You're sopping wet." Rudy's voice was muffled by my juicy cunt. He pressed his lips to my hot button, while at the same time dipping a finger into my sodden depths. Then he placed his lubed digit against my asshole and pushed it inside. I quivered with pleasure and moaned loudly.

"That's it, Rudy," I cried. "Fuck my tiny hole with your finger."

He pumped it in and out, going all the way to the knuckle with each thrust. Meanwhile, his tongue flicked across my swollen clit, faster and faster until I lost control and screamed into the wide blue sky as an orgasm ripped through me. Rudy replaced his finger with his tongue and rimmed my back door, making my climactic spasms go on even longer.

When at last I could catch my breath, I rolled over and lay flat on my stomach, embracing the asphalt. Its black, pebbly rough surface had been heated by the sun and felt uniquely pleasurable against my skin.

"There's lube in the pocket of my shorts," I called to Rudy. I never leave home without it.

He was back in a second. I didn't look, but I heard him strip off his shorts, and then there was only the sound of his quickened breathing while he applied the lube to his dick. I raised my hips, lifting my butt into the air. "Now fuck my ass," I rasped, sounding a little frantic. I was truly desperate to feel his cock penetrate me back there.

Rudy knelt behind me, and the next instant I felt the tip of his penis nudge my back hole. He placed his hands on my asscheeks in preparation for a forward thrust. I completed the job by lifting my rump sharply higher. Just like that his cockhead popped through my anal ring and filled up the space beyond.

Rudy grunted with exertion. I envied his ability to see it all, to watch in minute detail as his meaty shaft stretched my anus and vanished inside my body. He spread the orbs of my ass wider with his hands and leaned forward to drive deeper up my rear passage. I gasped with satisfaction, completely in tune with the sense of fullness I was feeling back there. My anal opening—tight but pliant—welcomed every inch of Rudy's shaft. When that lengthy spike was completely buried in my ass, Rudy squeezed my fleshy cheeks and then eased halfway out, only to drive home again. He began sawing in and out, cleaving my derriere with gusto. I loved every moment of his prick being inside me.

As I lurched and rocked under the force of my husband's eager thrusts, I remained aware of the uniqueness of our setting. It was easy to visualize cars rolling along here not too long ago, right where Rudy and I were enjoying our audacious anal fuck. It was easy to imagine that a car might *still* come along at any second.

Then my cravings reasserted themselves, blotting out all other thoughts. I yearned for the deepest, fullest anal sensations possible. Raising myself up onto all fours, I rocked back at Rudy. He stroked my hips and grabbed fistfuls of my hair as he pounded into my butt faster and faster. Soon I was moaning and screeching like a wildcat, and there wasn't anything I could do about it; I was in feral mode. Nobody could hear me anyway, except Rudy, of course, and my savage sounds only served to enflame his lust. He grabbed hold of my hips, jacked ferociously into my ass a dozen times more, and then released his load with a crazy animalistic cry of his own. I felt his cream spurt violently, far up inside my channel. The feeling triggered a massive climax for me, too. I pitched forward and back on my hands and knees, slamming backward against Rudy as my tiniest hole sought to siphon every last drop of his come. I was soon filled with an enormous volume of semen back there, so much so that when Rudy at last withdrew, a liberal amount of the white stuff leaked out and puddled on the road.

Rudy made good use of that encounter in his erotic writings, too. He never lets a good scene go to waste—and I make sure he's never stumped for ideas. It's a perfect relationship.

Erotic Eavesdropping

ALISON TYLER

"I slept with him."

I heard those words and stopped paying attention to my crossword puzzle. I was sitting in a burgundy leather booth at my favorite diner, sipping coffee and matching my wits against the puzzler in my local paper. So far, I'd been proud of my prowess. Now, I didn't care what the correct answer to sixteen across was. I found myself far more interested in the conversation occurring in the booth behind me.

"On the first date?" a second female voice queried.

The answer was not really a word. It was more of a sigh or a hum of delight. I looked to my right and caught a flash of the women's reflections in the diner window. The one with her back to my back had dark hair in a braid over one shoulder. The one across from her had curly red hair to her shoulders. The redhead was the one to lean in and say, "But you *never* fuck on the first date."

"I did last night."

"What got into you?"

"Roger." There was giggling.

"Yes, I get that. But what did he do to you?"

"He fucked me. Oh god, how he fucked me."

More giggling.

I pretended to continue doing the crossword, in case they were paying attention to my movements. But I didn't think I was on their radar. I started to write some of their key words into the small boxes of my puzzle.

"I mean," said the louder voice, "what did he *do* to get you to fuck him? You're always talking about how you have to really know a man before you let him in your bed."

"We didn't make it to my bed."

"Nora!"

"We didn't. We started having sex in the hallway outside of my apartment. He had my blouse open before I put the key in the lock. He got my bra undone before I turned the knob."

"So to speak."

"Touché."

"So tell," begged Nora's friend. "What made you give in so quickly? I've known you forever. You never do stuff like this."

"I know. That's what made it so fucking exciting."

"Fucking! Listen to you! The mouth on you. You never swear."

Nora still was laughing. The sound of sheer giddiness in her voice made me smile. I wished I knew the women. I wished I could sidle into their booth so that I could be an actual participant in their conversation.

"So tell," her friend continued. I was about to turn around and say, "Come on, Nora. Tell. What did Roger do to you?" when the waitress came over to refill my cup. Her eyes roved over my puzzle. FUCK.

I felt my cheeks go pink. She filled the coffee without a comment and moved on down the aisle. Nora, thankfully, didn't stop talking. She said, "He started in at dinner. He was telling me how he'd been enamored of me for years, and it was only because he'd landed a job at a different company that he could finally get up the nerve to ask me out."

"That's not an explanation."

"Well, the thing is…" She lowered her voice. I held myself entirely still. "The thing is that we played this game at dinner. He said he was going to tell me a fantasy, and I would tell him one. It felt really safe."

"So what was his fantasy?"

"To fuck me up the ass."

I spilled my coffee all over the sparkly red Formica table, but I snatched up my puzzle in the nick of time. The waitress came over quickly and mopped up the mess with a white-and-blue dishtowel. The look she gave me this time let me know she was listening to the conversation, as well. She refilled my cup and didn't say a word about the fact that my crossword puzzle was filled with words more appropriate for a bathroom wall. When she left, I added ANAL to a four-letter box. So "anal" wasn't the answer to an old-fashioned machine used for tilling. Though it sounded like Nora had gotten plowed to me.

"The thing is," Nora said again, "that was my fantasy as well. As soon as he said the words, I knew we were going to fuck."

"I can't believe you," Nora's friend said.

I could almost hear Nora shrug. "He said it in such a way, I knew we were going to do it. He promised to go slow. He explained that he would make me climax like I never had before. And then he made each of those promises come true."

That's when I pulled out my wallet and paid my bill, making sure to give a little more than I normally would have for the tip. I left the paper where it was and called my boyfriend as I walked from the diner. "I'm on my way over," I told Logan.

"Oh, good. I thought I wasn't going to see you until after lunch."

"Have the lube out when I get there."

There was a hesitation, then the husky sound of Logan clearing his throat. My man loves when we have anal sex. "Okay," he said. "I'll be ready."

I didn't know if I could make it to his place fast enough. I thought I might actually have a spontaneous orgasm on the drive to his house. I wondered if that would work as an excuse if an officer pulled me over. "I'm sorry I went through the yellow light, sir. I was coming." The entire ride, I replayed the women's conversation in my head. I loved the thought of these people I didn't know, had never met, having anal on the first date. Why? Simple. Because that's what Logan and I did.

I was about five miles away. Long enough for a trip down memory lane.

Logan and I had been set up by mutual friends. Our buddies were certain we'd hit it off. I was sure we wouldn't. I'd heard about Logan over the years. He was a musician. He drove a motorcycle. He was hipper than me. I usually don't go for rebels. But then we met, and there was something crazy about our initial connection. He was exactly my type in the looks department: long, thick black hair, blue eyes you could float a boat in, and full kissable lips. But I wasn't going to be had by a pretty face alone. I wanted more. Substance, depth, a connection.

When we shook hands, I felt a jolt to my core. So there was the chemical attraction. Over drinks—that's all I had agreed to—we found ourselves sharing intimate details of our past relationships. And when, at some point, his thigh bumped against mine at the restaurant, I felt my pussy tighten. The conversation lasted past drinks and into a late dinner. The discussion went from confessional to what I can only describe as pure foreplay. I'd been toying with the fringe on my dress as I said, "What's your favorite way to fuck?"

"I'm a backdoor man," he told me.

We left the restaurant minutes later.

I was almost to his house now, and I kept thinking of what had happened that night. He'd taken me to his place, and he'd undressed me in his bedroom. He'd gone slowly at first, as if unsure that I really was ready to do this. I'd had to slather up his cock with lube and bend over for him, insisting that yes, I am an anal-hound all the way. I love anal sex. It's the one way I know I'll always get off. The only way I truly feel fulfilled.

Logan had primed me with his cock in my pussy first, then he had parted my cheeks and pushed his dickhead against my tight hole.

My key was in the lock now. No more reminiscing. There was Logan, on the sofa. He had spread out towels on the carpet, put music on the stereo, and there was the lube. Waiting.

I was stripping out of my clothes almost before I kicked the door shut. Logan looked surprised by my actions, but he didn't appear anything but happy. He stood and pulled his white T-shirt over his head, then went to work on his black jeans. When we were both naked, he took me in his arms and kissed me. I could feel how hard his dick was. I reached down and stroked him, and he shivered. "I got a hard-on as soon as you said 'lube,'" he told me.

"I knew you would."

I reached for the bottle and poured a generous amount of the glistening liquid into my palm. Logan stood still while I wrapped my greasy fist around his fine dick and began to work him. He was fully erect and felt fierce in my hand. I lubed him up generously, knowing that the more grease I got on his cock, the smoother the ride would be for me. But I wasn't content to merely let my fingers do the talking. I said, "I almost came on the way over, fantasizing."

"Tell me," he insisted.

I handed him the lube and bent over in front of him. He used the lubrication to oil up my asshole. I reached back and held my cheeks wide apart for him so he could get in really deep. He let one thumb flicker over my opening, and I cried out. Logan knows how totally sensitive my rosebud is. He knows that if he touches me in the perfect way, I can come from anal stimulation alone. Hell, I can practically come from thinking about having him fuck my back door.

"You like it," Logan said in a low, raw voice as he prepped my rear hole.

"Yes," I hissed between my teeth.

I was desperate for him to start fucking me. He was clearly more interested in taking things slow. I've never been good at slow. I like fast and hard. "Put it in me," I demanded.

"There's no rush," Logan insisted. Clearly, he had not been the one eavesdropping on the sexy conversation at the diner. There was most definitely a rush. I was desperate to feel his fabulous cock in my asshole.

"But I'm so ready," I said, and I knew I sounded pouty and petulant, but I couldn't help myself. I needed Logan's cock inside me. I looked at him over my shoulder. I tried to make my eyes look sensual and inviting. "Come on, baby," I said, trying to be seductive. "Let me feel your big, fat cock in my tight little hole."

Logan didn't fall for my tricks.

He slid his cock forward as if he were going to pierce me. Then at the last possible moment he dipped down to enter my pussy. I practically screamed *No!*, but I knew better. Logan is a tease. As much as he likes anal, he also likes to make me wait. He made me wait now, fucking my slippery pussy in nice, even strokes. He even brought one hand between my legs to tickle my clit while he fucked me, as if giving me a consolation prize for not simply reaming my ass from the start.

Actually, his motions *were* working on me. I felt myself starting to melt for him. He rubbed his knuckles roughly up and over my clit, and I said, "Oh, fuck, I'm going to…Logan, I'm going to come."

He'd apparently been waiting for my words, because as soon as I spoke, he was in motion. He moved his hand from my clit, grabbed hold of my asscheeks, and pulled them wide open. His cock hesitated for one brief second, and then he was in. Oh, sweet heaven, he was in me.

I braced myself with my hands on the coffee table, and I arched my back like a bow. Logan drove in hard, and as he did, he said, "You're so damn tight. I love how you feel." I came almost instantly around his dick. My asshole squeezed him in a series of contractions that was practically obscene in strength. I'd been ready to climax for nearly an hour. I went off in a major way—and all the time I pictured Nora exploring anal, giving in to her basest desires. My body was wracked with the pleasure. I felt as if I was experiencing a double-orgasm—one in my pussy and one in my asshole.

Logan was just getting started. He seemed to appreciate the way my body responded to him, and he held still for a moment, allowing me to eke out every last ripple of pleasure. Then he started to fuck me in the most divine rhythm. Leave it to a musician to be able to incorporate the beat of the music into the way he was fucking me. In, out, in and out to the sounds pulsing from the speakers. I realized right then that he'd chosen a record with a throbbing bass. He must have imagined what our actions would be like before I'd even arrived.

While he fucked me, I continued to let myself envision Nora and her Roger—whoever they were. I thought of what it felt like to be taken anally for the first time by a new partner. There was always a little bit of a learning curve. I wondered if Roger had remembered to use plenty of lube. I wondered if Nora had parted her own cheeks or let her new lover hold her open himself. I could feel how wet my pussy was growing at these thoughts.

In fact, when Logan pushed in hard enough to make me moan, I almost called out the name Roger. That let me know I needed to release the fantasy and pay more attention to my flesh-and-blood lover behind me. I shook back my hair and looked over my shoulder at him. "That feels so good," I said.

"I know."

"You're going to make me come again if you keep working me like that," I said next.

"Then I'd better keep working you like that," he said, and he began to fuck me even harder, even faster. I brought one hand off the coffee table to stroke my clit while Logan drove in deep. Logan didn't mind that. He was using both of his hands to hold my cheeks apart so he could watch his cock go in and out of my rear hole. When the pleasure flooded me once more, I practically came unhinged. I cried out so loud that I muffled the sounds against my right arm, not wanting any of Logan's neighbors to come banging on the front door. Not while Logan was in my back door!

Only after my orgasm had subsided did Logan reach his own limits. He gripped me tightly by the hips, slammed his body to mine, and shot his load deep inside me. His body jerked with spasm after spasm as he filled me up with his seed. Together, we collapsed against the coffee table, drinking the air in with hungry breaths, completely demolished by the ride. I was shiny with sweat, my hair slicked against my face and the back of my neck, my whole body trembling as if I'd just finished a monster workout. Logan looked as decimated as I felt.

We sat next to each other, listening to the music for a few moments, both of us pleased with what had just occurred. When we'd recovered, Logan led me to the bathroom and we settled into his Jacuzzi tub for a shared bubble bath.

"What got into you this morning?" he asked as he sudsed me all over.

"Nora and Roger and the crossword," I said, thinking of how Nora had answered a similar question earlier in the morning. Then I confessed to eavesdropping on the women at the diner.

"What did they look like?" Logan wanted to know.

I'd only been able to spy on them in the window and glance quickly when I walked by on my way out of the restaurant. But I was able to fill Logan in with the basic details. "Nora had thick black hair that she was wearing in a braid."

"Mmm," Logan sighed, and he nudged me with one of his feet, angling to stroke me between my legs. "I like braids. Good for pulling." I sat back against one of the jets and wriggled with pleasure.

"Her friend was a redhead," I said, "but I never learned her name."

"I love anonymous redheads."

"And they were talking anal sex—all before they had breakfast."

"I love anal before…"

I splashed him. That started a water fight that ended up in Logan grabbing me in his arms and facing my body so that one of the jets was spraying directly on my pussy. I felt as if I might dissolve under the steady beat. The jets were sublime, providing the perfect amount of clit stimulation. I wasn't surprised at all to feel Logan's cock getting erect again. I also wasn't surprised to feel him wedging himself between my cheeks.

"You spread your pussy lips," he said. "Let the spray really work you good."

I did what he said, maneuvering into a position in which I felt as if I were being fucked by the steady stream of water. Since we'd already had anal, my back door was plenty primed and ready. But Logan made sure by working his pointer finger into my hole and gently stroking me on the inside.

I held on to the lip of the tub, preparing to feel Logan in my ass once more. But he surprised me. "Let yourself come," he said, "and then I'm going to take your ass again."

I came practically on his words, repeating his name over and over like a mantra. Logan spun me around and held my cheeks very wide apart. The spray from the jet pounded against my asshole. I sucked in a great gulp of air and then let it out again in a moan.

"Do you like that?"

"Oh god, yes."

"What do you want?"

"I want you to fuck my ass again."

"How do you want me to fuck you?"

"Hard," I whimpered. "So hard."

Logan maneuvered me once more, and this time he insinuated his cock between my asscheeks and pressed my pussy against the spray. I was limp and relaxed, buffeted on the water and his cock. The bliss of the motions ricocheted inside me. I felt not as if I was going to come again, but as if I might never stop.

"Later on," Logan said in a low voice, "we'll go out to the diner, and we'll talk all about the anal we had."

"And maybe," I panted, "maybe someone at the next booth will overhear and go home to his or her partner."

"It will be like a chain reaction," Logan whispered as he came, grinding his hips to my ass and pushing me into the spray. "Anal sex happening all over the city."

My fingers searched for purchase on the lip of the tub as the final climax of the morning fell over me. I slid back in the bath against Logan, and I closed my eyes.

We'd had anal like never before—and all because of a morning coffee and a crossword.

Now, what was the correct answer to sixteen across?

Intimate Explorations

Hope Garner

My friend Candace is an empathic, nurturing person, so when she started talking about pursuing a part-time career in massage therapy, I encouraged her to go for it. Eventually she took my advice and enrolled in massage school—and then I realized I was in trouble. It was only a matter of time before Candi would ask to practice on me. And when that happened, I'd have to confront my secret desires. Could *you* lie still and do nothing while the object of your private sexual fantasies ran her hands all over your naked body? I was pretty sure I couldn't. Even if I tried, I wouldn't fool Candi, who is as intuitive as she is good-looking. (Yes, my friend is beautiful, with hazel eyes, a mane of dark-brown hair, creamy skin, and a lovely hourglass figure.) Candi arouses my carnal passions even in the most mundane circumstances. A full-body massage would be off-the-charts intolerable. She would detect my sexual response to her touch, and she would know the truth. What would happen to our relationship? I was afraid to find out—and, on a deeper level, afraid not to, especially since I'd sensed that the interest might be mutual. Our friendship was a close one, and recently there had been subtle hints of flirtation that seemed to be occurring with greater frequency.

One month into her training at the institute, Candi called and suggested the inevitable. "Come over to my place Friday afternoon," she said, explaining that she wanted to practice on me for a full hour. "I bought a massage table yesterday. Picked up a bunch of aromatherapy oils, too. I can't wait to try everything."

The thought of putting her off made me face the truth: I *wanted* to feel Candi's hands on me. I thought of her pouring warm oil onto my skin and rubbing it in as I lay nude on her massage table. My private reverie had no room for a sheet draped over my private parts. I could almost feel Candi's fingers sliding up the backs of my thighs, up over the swells of my asscheeks—and into the cleft between. She would glean from my body's reactions not just that I was aroused, but also that she had found my favorite erogenous zone. When I'm with a lover, or even by myself with my drawer full of sex toys, nothing sets me off quite like anal play. I imagined Candi's touch on my firm, round bottom, her fingers kneading the muscles before slipping into my crack to probe my sensitive rear opening.

"Hope? Are we on for Friday?" came Candi's voice on the phone.

"Oh, sorry," I said, realizing I had gone silent for several seconds. My cunt was damp from my brief fantasy. "Yes. We're on."

I thought about little else until Friday came around. Thirty minutes before the appointed time, I showered and groomed my blonde pubic mound with a razor. Then I donned a casual dress and sandals. There didn't seem any point for underwear on this occasion, so I didn't bother. Walking over to Candi's apartment two blocks away, I felt deliciously indecent and sexy, but also nervous. *It's just a massage*, I reminded myself. But I kept thinking of the masseuse in question, and of my dirty daydream, and I became more and more turned on.

Candi had arranged her living room beautifully for the occasion. The blinds were drawn, and scented candles flickered everywhere. New Age music played softly on hidden surround-sound speakers. In the center of the room, the massage table waited. It looked like a professional model, with a padded face cradle at one end. I spotted an assortment of massage oils on a side table. My nipples stiffened with arousal, and my sex began to drip in earnest.

"Thanks for letting me practice on you," Candi said. Barefoot, she wore a white T-shirt and loose-fitting shorts. I had a sudden impulse—not for the first time—to yank her clothes off and pull her to me. Candi's butt, so full and shapely, is the highlight of her considerable physical assets; no baggy shorts could diminish it.

She indicated a chair nearby, saying, "You can put your clothes there. When you're undressed, go ahead and lie on the table, facedown. I'll give you a minute." She left the room.

I took a deep breath, then kicked off my sandals and pulled off my dress. The massage table was fitted with a soft white sheet that Candi had pre-warmed in her clothes dryer. Another sheet, folded neatly in a rectangle, lay on top. It was obviously meant to cover my butt after I lay down.

I thought back to my wicked reverie and reached a decision.

When Candi came back into the room, she found me lying on my stomach on the table, as she had instructed. But the covering sheet was on the floor, not on me. She stopped in her tracks, assessing the situation. Had the sheet slipped off accidentally? I could feel her eyes on me, surveying my bare rump. After a moment, her footsteps approached. I heard the rustle of the sheet as she picked it up from the floor. Disappointed, I waited to feel the fabric settle over my backside. But she seemed to be thinking it over.

"I suppose we don't really need to use this," Candi said at last. "This is a private massage between friends. In this situation there's no reason for you to be draped, unless you want to be. Do you, Hope?"

I summoned my courage and said, "No. You can leave it off." In for a penny, in for a pound.

She opened a bottle of massage oil and poured a liberal amount of the fragrant liquid between my shoulder blades. Then she began rubbing my back and shoulders. It felt incredibly good. Rather than slip into a relaxed state, though, I found my arousal increasing, exactly as I had anticipated. It didn't matter where she touched me—my hands, arms, feet, calves; she got around to them all—I simply grew more and more revved up. At one point her fingers grazed the sides of my breasts, and I squirmed with pleasure. She didn't acknowledge my agitated state, but she did pause to get a different bottle of oil. "This one doubles as a personal lube," she said, with a giggle that sounded a little tense. *So,* I thought, *you're keyed up, too.*

"You have a lovely body," Candi murmured as she worked on my left leg. "I've always thought so, but seeing you this way and feeling you with my hands confirms it. You're so toned and firm. Such beautiful skin, too." Her fingers moved in slow figure eights along the back of my thigh, inching ever closer to my ass. I felt a tremor in my sex that was small but potent. My juices were leaking out, dampening my inner thighs and the sheet beneath me. I longed for Candi's touch there—between my labia, yes, but especially around back, between my asscheeks. Her hands crept along in that direction, driving me mad. I stifled a moan and spread my thighs farther apart. Candi kept kneading my flesh as if she hadn't noticed, but she had to notice when I did it again, this time lifting my hips slightly off the table. After that, her touch seemed to become more sensual, more erotic. Excitedly I lifted my ass a tiny bit higher, which parted my cheeks a little. Candi's hands reached the top of my leg. Slowly, meticulously, she stroked that sublime juncture where thigh meets buttcheek. After a minute, though, she moved to my right leg, leaving me terribly frustrated. I had to acknowledge that perhaps my needs were not the same as Candi's.

Or was I wrong? She was moving a little quicker now, up my right calf to the back of my knee and beyond, pouring out more of the massage oil/lube as she worked her way along my thigh. At last she arrived at my ass again. I felt more liquid dribble directly onto my cheeks, followed by the touch of Candi's hands as she began kneading my bottom. It was happening just like in my fantasy. My body trembled and I whimpered, no longer caring if Candi knew what was happening to me. Her hands were working my buttocks, grabbing them, spreading them. Desperate, I shifted my hips suddenly, which propelled Candi's fingers into my asscrack. One fingertip grazed my anus; her thumb came to rest on my perineum.

"Oh, yes!" I cried, unable to withstand the force of my lust. For a gut-wrenching moment, I feared Candi might snatch her hand away and call off the whole session, but my fear was baseless. She palmed the well-oiled spheres of my ass firmly and aggressively while her fingers played in my dark crevasse. Leaning down, she whispered in my ear, "You're a dirty, naughty girl, aren't you?" I nodded and lifted my head from the cradle to glance at her. Candi's eyes burned with passion. "You love to have your ass played with," she continued. "I understand that now. I know something about ass play, too. Do you like this?"

She began rotating her thumb around the rim of my puckered orifice, which made me squirm wildly with pleasure. At the same time, she slipped two fingers into my sopping cunt, which accepted her digits gladly. But it was my ass that was really grooving, sending out sparks of sensation that made me light-headed. Candi's thumb traced ever-tightening circles around my tiniest hole, spiraling into the bull's-eye. I felt myself on the edge of losing control.

"I know you're close, I can feel it," Candi murmured, her lips close to my ear. "Come for me, Hope. Let yourself go." Her thumb was directly on my sphincter, insistently rubbing and pressing that elastic ring of muscle. "You have such a nice ass," Candi breathed. "It's pulling me in." As she spoke I felt her thumb push through my back door and into the warm space beyond. A moment later, her entire digit was buried snugly inside my ass. My other senses began to fade away as my mind and body focused wholly on Candi's wriggling thumb. I felt my anus relaxing, acclimating itself to my friend's manual intrusion. She felt it, too, and added another finger there, and then a third, having abandoned my cunt to slide her well-lubed digits slowly but steadily into my grateful ass. I felt incredibly stretched and stuffed back there. When she started pushing in and out with a corkscrew motion, orgasmic explosions of light and heat ripped through me, shaking me to the core. Candi kept at it, bringing me off time and time again until

I was nearly delirious. It might have lasted a minute or an hour; I lost all sense of time.

"Oh my, where did you learn to do that?" I said at last, panting heavily as I sat up.

"You're not the only one who loves anal sex," Candi said, and she kissed me full on the lips.

"You lie down now," I demanded, eager to give my companion an equally stimulating massage. She grinned and quickly stripped bare. I couldn't help staring at her lovely breasts, her slender waist, her full hips, and her nearly bald cunt. Her eyes shone brightly with desire, and I knew mine did, too, because I was still completely turned on, a slave to my lust.

Candi stretched out on her stomach on the massage table, providing me with my first good look at her butt. What a sumptuous ass it was, so fleshy and round. I couldn't wait to ply her sensitive rear hole. First things first, however. I wanted to take my full measure of her body.

The dual-purpose lubricant she had been using on me was already one-third gone. I upended the bottle and poured a copious amount into my cupped hands, which I then applied to Candi's voluptuous frame. Starting at her shoulders, I worked my way down her back but then skipped over her ass, which made her whimper with desperation. I resumed the massage at her feet and traveled up her sexy legs, just as she had done with me. Her butt, so very tempting, was an inch or two from my fingertips, but I simply said, "Turn over, please."

Candi did as I asked. Her erect nipples, creamy torso, and coffee-colored wisp of pubic hair made my mouth water. I slathered a generous amount of oil onto her chest and rubbed it all over her shapely breasts. Sliding my hands downward over her belly, I made sure every square inch of Candi's smooth skin was slick and shiny. She quivered and moaned softly, with her eyes closed. Finally, I reached her pubic mound and spent a moment toying with the tiny patch of curls. Just below, the lips of her sex were swollen and wet. Impatient, Candi pulled her knees back almost to her ears, which lifted her ass off the table and exposed her tiniest orifice. I decided it was time to get down to business. First, I squirted a stream of the massage liquid directly onto her taut asscheeks. Then I spread the stuff across her skin and into her crack, to the very rim of her anus. Candi trembled, anxious to feel me probe her clenching hole. In another second I obliged her, pressing my index finger against her asshole and then burrowing through. I leaned in to watch closely; I'm sure Candi could feel my rapid breaths on her skin.

She gave a cry of excitement that grew louder as I pushed my finger farther up her rear channel. With my other hand, I massaged the soft folds of her pussy, which were deliciously slick. She reached down, grabbed one of her asscheeks and pulled it away from the other, widening her crack and inviting me to fill her back passage more completely. I lubed up another finger and carefully slid it in beside the first, feeling her sphincter muscle flex and expand. "Oh yeah, my god, that's good..." Her words were less articulate after that; she started writhing in ecstasy. The table rattled with her motions. I continued to massage her pussy and decided to see if she could accommodate one more finger between her cheeks. She did so, eagerly. "I'm coming!" she shrieked as my third digit disappeared into her anus. She was rocking back and forth so severely that she propelled my fingers in and out of her clutching asshole with almost no help from me. Her orgasm lasted at least as long as mine had, and when she was finished, her entire body was flushed.

Candi sat up and swung her legs off the table. The look we exchanged made it abundantly clear that both of us wanted to take our anal explorations to the next level. "Let's take a shower," she suggested, and I nodded. We hurried into her shower together and rinsed the massage oil from each other's bodies. After we'd dried each other, Candi jumped onto her bed and turned to welcome me into her arms. Her breasts, full and free, squashed up against my smaller ones as we kissed. My primal urges began to assert themselves again, compelling me to push Candi flat on the bed and climb atop her, facing her feet.

"Put your fingers back in my ass," Candi demanded. She was insatiable. Thanks to our earlier adventure, her anus still felt relaxed and pliable. I lubed up three fingers and gradually inserted all of them, acting more confidently this time, and taking pleasure in the way Candi twisted and moaned. When I was sure she was ready, I began pumping my fingers in and out of her bottom. She did the same to me, manually plundering my backside aggressively until my breath came in short, rapid gasps. Her juicy sex was right below my face, so I lowered my head and slid my tongue between her plump pussy lips. Candi followed suit, eating my sex with surprising relish. There were plenty of surprises to go around that day.

After a minute I withdrew my fingers and tried probing my companion's crack with my tongue. "Ooh, yes, baby," she said, trembling uncontrollably. "Lick my hole." The words were no sooner out of her mouth than she started in on me, too, massaging my back door with the flat of her tongue. The feeling was exquisite. I wiggled my hips and rocked backward, encouraging her to probe my asshole. She cooed and thrust her tongue between my buttocks, sampling my tiny orifice. In return I rimmed her anus thoroughly, then dashed the tip of my tongue through her puckered opening. I felt her sphincter rapidly clench and release as the climactic sensations built up within her body. All the while I let my fingers play in the sticky depths of Candi's cunt, occasionally teasing her clit between my finger and thumb.

For several minutes we undulated against each other, alternating fingers and tongues as we probed the forbidden recesses of each other's asses. Finally, Candi dropped her head back to the mattress and asked me to retrieve a dildo and lube from her nightstand drawer, which was within my reach. I opened the drawer and found an impressive collection of toys, mostly designed for anal play. I selected a fat pink dildo and a small packet of lube for Candi and tossed them to her, then grabbed some thick anal lube and a long black toy for me to use on her. She eyed the toy in my hand, grinned salaciously, and squirmed out from under me. I rolled onto my back, and we resumed our sixty-nine position with Candi on top this time. Her supple body was no sooner prostrate upon mine, her thighs on either side of my head, than I felt her slicked-up dildo enter my ass. Smoothly, steadily, it tunneled right up my back passage, making me feel deliciously full. I gasped, immersed for a moment in the sensations, and then I greased up the black toy and positioned it at Candi's rear entrance. Her ass was spread beautifully above my face and the little hole winked at me, eager for action. Candi's moan of anticipation became a sigh of blissful pleasure as I pushed the glossy dildo through her sphincter. Slowly, I shoved it in deeper, until nothing but the flared base remained visible between her cheeks. Taking firm hold of it, I eased the whole length back out, then crammed it in again, making Candi pant with delight.

In mere seconds, we were engaged in a contest to see who could fuck the other's ass faster, harder, deeper. Candi came first, crying out with unspeakable pleasure until she broke down in sobs of joy. While she was still riding high, I experienced my own climax, the force of which made me twist to and fro like a wild animal beneath Candi. I raked my free hand over the taut curve of her asscheeks while the fever of bliss ran its course.

In the end, our anal tryst didn't harm the relationship between Candi and me at all. Our friendship not only survived, it thrived—morphing into something greater, deeper, and more intimate. We weren't merely friends after that. We were lovers.

Backdoor Blind Date

MARA MACINTOSH

When my friend Sabrina set me up with her coworker Bryan, I wasn't sure what I expected out of the evening, but I knew how I'd have liked it to end—with his cock buried balls-deep in my ass. Anal sex had been a fantasy of mine for a long time, one I hadn't had the chance to act on with my last boyfriend, Dave.

Dave and I dated for more than a year and had a pretty satisfying sex life except for fulfilling that one desire of mine. It was as much my fault as Dave's. I hadn't been open about my wish until near the end of our relationship. I'd been afraid he wouldn't find the idea as erotic and exciting as I did, so I'd used dildos and vibrators to simulate the experience on my own, but they didn't have the same appeal as a real cock.

When I'd finally come out and told Dave what I wanted instead of merely hinting by jutting my ass up into the air, Dave let me know he didn't share my interest. It was yet another indicator that we weren't as well matched as we'd once thought. I made the decision to cut my losses and set out in search of a relationship that would make me truly happy.

On my own and ready to date again, I decided that whomever I next had sex with, I'd make my desires known from the beginning. This blind date set up by Sabrina was my first chance to test that resolve. No holding back, no hesitation—I was going to get laid the way I wanted. I hoped Bryan would turn out to be the guy who could scratch my particular itch.

The date wasn't completely "blind." I'd met Bryan before at one of Sabrina's parties. I'd noticed he was sexy and he seemed nice, but that was all the attention I'd paid him at the time since I was still with Dave.

Once I was single, Sabrina filled me in on the details about Bryan. I already knew I found him attractive, so I was ready to take a chance.

We met at a restaurant where we lingered over drinks and dinner for so long that we missed our movie. I wasn't really interested in seeing the flick anyway, and I could tell he wasn't either. We found we had a lot in common. He was easy to talk to and even easier on the eyes. But more importantly, there was a kind of electric current that crackled in the air between us. Without a word being spoken, we both knew we'd be having sex before the evening was over.

Post-dinner drinks lasted until the question of "your place or mine?" was posed. Bryan's apartment was closer, so we drove there. We barely made it into the foyer of the building before grabbing at each other. Bryan was a tall, lanky guy who easily lifted me off my feet when he pulled me against him.

I eagerly wrapped my legs around his hips, and he pressed me up against the bank of mailboxes in the lobby. The little handles dug into my back, while Bryan's erection nudged my crotch. I rubbed my pussy up and down the bulge in his jeans and eagerly opened my mouth to his aggressive kisses. After an evening of teasing, talking, and foot play underneath the restaurant table, my pussy was wet and ready, but my asshole was also clenching at the possibility of my erotic dream being fulfilled.

One of the other tenants came through the front door in a billow of icy air, interrupting our passionate groping. Coming to his senses, Bryan set me down on my feet, and we hurriedly climbed the stairs to his third-floor apartment.

I accepted the cabernet he offered and sipped it slowly as I looked around the place, but I wasn't really interested in drinking or the décor. Happily, my date wasn't either. Wineglasses abandoned, we were soon back in each other's arms, kissing, touching, and straining to get closer. He pulled off my top. I unfastened his pants. He flipped the clasp on my bra. I popped the buttons on his shirt. When we were both finally naked, he carried me to his bedroom.

I sprawled across the mattress, watching him rummage through the nightstand for condoms, and searched for the words to ask for what I wanted. Finally, I decided to drop obvious clues, like guiding his cock to my asshole, rather than utter my request out loud. It turned out I didn't have to either ask or prompt him because Bryan made the first move.

As he lay facing me, his hand slipped around my waist to caress my ass, while his cock rubbed rhythmically against my crotch, building a warm, steady glow in my clit. He kissed my mouth, my neck, and my breasts, and all the while his hand kept kneading my cheeks. Then his finger slid between them and brushed over my anus, a delicate touch that set a fire raging through me.

I squeezed my buttocks tight, not in rejection but in eager anticipation. I moaned softly so he'd know I liked it. He nudged more intensely, worrying the puckered opening while his mouth tugged on my nipple. The triple sensation of his suckling mouth, hard cock, and probing finger had my body burning. I pushed back against his digit, encouraging his entry, and I moaned as the ring of muscle relaxed around his fingertip.

Bryan withdrew his finger, slicked it up with lube from a bottle on his nightstand, and carefully slipped his digit into my anus. First one finger and then two were stretching me wider, and then pushing in and out. The sensation was incredibly sexy. As he fucked me slowly, he guided his cock to my cunt and filled me there as well. The double penetration made me gasp with pleasure.

Bryan's lips had completely abandoned my tits as he concentrated on fucking me front and back. It wasn't quite the action I'd imagined, but it felt so good I didn't mind. Besides, we had the rest of the night, and I knew my complete fantasy would come true before it was over.

Initially, he'd eased his fingers inside me, letting my back hole get accustomed to their girth, but as excitement overtook him, he pushed them in as deep as he could. I rocked forward and back, accepting him inside me in both openings. The only thing that would have made it even hotter was a cock filling my mouth, too. But Bryan's mouth covered mine and his tongue acted the part, plunging in time with his dick.

I moaned louder, my pleasure too great to hold back. Just as I reached my peak and shuddered against him, Bryan's fingers and cock plunged hard one last time and froze. His fingers were jammed deep inside my ass, and his cock throbbed in my cunt with his release.

I pulled away from his ferocious kiss to gasp for breath as I came down from my climax. Afterward, we both collapsed on the bed, limp and relieved. No longer shy, I admitted to Bryan that anal sex had long been an erotic fantasy of mine. He assured me he'd be happy to satisfy my craving after he'd had a chance to recover.

We took a moment to clean up, and then lay down again. Bryan asked if I'd like to watch some backdoor action to get me even more in the mood. When I saw his adult DVD collection, I knew I'd found my perfect match.

The movie he'd selected had a vague plot that quickly led to the characters stripping and fucking. The small-breasted blonde in the video begged for an ass-reaming and the dark-haired stud gave it to her. The man's hands held her cheeks spread wide so the camera could get a good shot of the action. Watching her puckered rosebud stretch wide around his thick cock was the hottest thing I'd ever seen.

The heat between my legs was fierce, and my pulse seemed to be centered there. I was flushed from the wine and the erotic content of the film. I glanced over at Bryan and saw his cock was hard again, his eyes riveted on the whimpering woman on the screen. I was ready to act out the very same role.

Bryan exchanged a look with me and growled an order, telling me to get on my hands and knees. I happily complied, assuming the position in the middle of his big bed. He slapped my ass and told me to raise it higher, and the heat from his hand only made me more turned on. His rough treatment was exactly what I wanted.

I lowered my face to my forearms and lifted my ass as high as it could go. He squirted a dollop of lubricant on his fingers and worked the cool gel into my hole. Once more his fingers spread me wide and then wider; three fingers this time, stretching me open in preparation for his cock. They slipped in and out easily with the help of the lube. I groaned at the pressure; it was just enough discomfort to amp up my arousal.

And then there was a pause, and the fingers were swiftly replaced with the head of his cock. He eased inside, and I dug my knees into the bed as Bryan's weight settled against my thighs. He pushed deeper, and the burning heat increased as my asshole stretched around his girth. He gripped my hips and thrust forward.

I moaned at the intense sensation and reached between my legs to finger my clit, adding a more immediate gratification to the deeper pleasure of being ass-fucked.

"Tell me what it feels like," I gasped, as he pulled out and thrust again, deeper than the first time.

"So fucking tight and hot," he grunted.

I imagined how it must feel—my inner muscles wrapped like a second skin around his cock, tighter than my pussy could ever be. As he moved in and out, the friction created an incredible heat. My body adjusted to accept the thickness of his cock, but the passion between us continued to build.

I kept my touch on my clit light, steadily building the tension while I waited to feel Bryan near his climax. He plowed into me faster and harder, grunting with the effort, our bodies slapping together loudly. With my chest pressed to the bed and my rear in the air, I enjoyed the feeling of submission the position gave me. And I loved the strength of his powerful thrusts.

Before long, I felt my partner reach his goal. With a harsh groan and a firm grip of my hips, he drove into me one last time. My finger flew in little circles on my clit, coaxing the climax that was ready to burst forth. Points of light danced behind my closed eyelids and delight sparkled through me. The mattress muffled my long moan as I came.

Bryan's hot, heavy weight against my back was the anchor that drew me down to earth. He rolled to the side, freeing my trapped body. I rose from the bed to clean up and returned to flop on my back with a sigh of contentment.

"Now that's what I'm talkin' about," I said softly, before smiling at Bryan.

"I'm glad you liked it," he said, returning my smile.

For a moment we both watched the television screen where the blonde was being fucked fore and aft by a couple of different guys. Her mouth was full of cock and her ass was receiving another reaming. We enjoyed watching the rest of the movie as my mind began to concoct more wicked scenarios for us to enact in the future.

As I'd hoped, my first date with Bryan was only the beginning of our sensual experimentation. We'd both finally found someone with compatible interests in the bedroom as well as outside of it.

The next time, I invited him to my apartment. I cooked dinner, a rare occurrence in my kitchen. After we ate and talked for a while, we made out, which ultimately ended with us fucking like wild things.

Bryan bent me over the back of the couch, my face planted in the cushions and my feet planted on the floor. With his hand on the back of my neck and my ass lifted, he nudged my legs farther apart, grasped my cheeks and pulled them wide. Cool air caressed my naked rear and my thighs quivered. My anus clenched and released in little spasms as I anxiously waited for his touch.

He surprised me. It wasn't his finger that lightly traced the puckered opening, but something warm and wet—his tongue. My pussy was sopping wet and clenching, too, and I nearly came at the unexpected, seductive caress. My entire body trembled in eagerness as his tongue lapped at my hole a few times, then probed a little way inside. I whined and my pulse thundered in my ears.

The soft caresses around and inside my entrance continued until I was shaky and on the verge of coming. Then I felt a wet kiss on each cheek of my ass, and Bryan's lust-roughened voice asked, "Do you have a dildo? Want to be double fucked?"

Cream dripped from my aching cunt at the mere suggestion. I told him where to find my toys, and then waited in my submissive position while he went to get what he needed.

My calf muscles quivered, but I kept my legs a shoulder width apart, exactly as he'd placed me. I listened to the sounds of Bryan rummaging through my toy box, and I wondered what he would choose to use on me. The anticipation added zest to an already intensely erotic situation.

When Bryan returned to the living room, I glanced toward him, but he commanded me not to look. "It's a surprise." So I only glimpsed part of his torso as he walked past—his groin with his erect cock jutting out before him like a ship's prow. I swallowed hard and eagerly waited for what would happen next.

Behind me, I heard little sounds as Bryan moved around, and then the familiar cool moisture as lubricant was smeared down my crack and rubbed into my hole. Blood throbbed in my temples from having my head down for so long, and the dizzy disorientation heightened my senses. Every sound, every slight brush of skin against my own, the musk of sex in the air and even the smell of my dusty couch, seemed stronger, more potent than normal. The ache of my straining legs and bowed back, the scrape of the couch upholstery against my erect nipples, it all vibrated through me. I wanted even more sensation, more stimulation—and when I heard the buzz of a vibrator I knew I was going to get it.

Bryan teased me with the faux cock, pressing the tip to my sensitive inner thighs and running it all around the edges of my cunt, which ached to be filled. I thought I'd explode as he continued to play with my body. He slipped the buzzing vibrator between the lips of my pussy, and then took it quickly away. He teased me in every way possible until I realized what he wanted: he wanted me to beg.

"Please. Please fuck me, now!" I was so desperate for relief that tears blurred my vision.

"What do you want?" He pressed the vibrator to my pussy again, letting it linger at the opening.

"To be fucked."

"How?"

"Your cock in my ass. That vibrator in my cunt."

Bryan gave a satisfied grunt, and then he finally gave me what I wanted. He plunged the vibrator fast and hard into my pussy. I gasped as it completely filled me.

I imagined how it looked to him, the thick toy disappearing into my depths. He pumped the vibrator in and out a couple of times, then he left it buried deep, while he pulled my cheeks apart and positioned his cockhead at my anus.

Even well lathered with slick lube, it was a tight fit. He pushed hard to get past the constricted ring of muscle, and once he was inside, he kept advancing. The first time we'd done this, he'd eased his way in, but this time Bryan was relentless in his pursuit.

I whimpered as he powered his way into my ass and my body molded around him. I cried out into the cushions, at first begging him to slow down, and then begging him to pound me harder.

The purring vibrator filled my cunt, and the live male cock plugged my rear. The combination was beyond anything I'd dreamed. In my position, my movement was limited. I couldn't thrust back; I could only accept whatever he gave me. The release of control was completely exhilarating.

I remained stock-still as he sheathed his dick to the hilt in my ass, then slowly drew it back out. My muscles gripped his shaft, refusing to let go of the solid length of his dick.

With a deep groan, Bryan thrust again. And then he began a rhythm, his cock moving in, while he pulled the vibrator out, the hard plastic pushing deep while his warm cock receded.

I was moaning continuously, whimpering and squirming. It was so intense, so deeply fulfilling, I didn't know how long I could stand it. I came and came again, one orgasm melting into another until I was a raw, open nerve. I kept beseeching Bryan, but I didn't know what for—to fuck me more or to stop and give me respite. "Please, please, please," I begged.

One last swift thrust and a shout marked Bryan's climax. He dropped the vibrator to the floor and grabbed my ass as his cock pulsed inside me.

The couch cushion beneath my face was wet with tears by the time we were finished. I was wrung out, exhausted, and completely satisfied. An occasional aftershock burst in my pussy like a firecracker. My ass was sore and my muscles felt strained. But the well-used feeling was perversely satisfying for me.

Bryan and I met many times after that and played many other sexual games, but my initiation into ass play was an experience I'll never forget.

Deep Hunger

KYLE HASKELL

"Why *not* just put it in my ass?" That question was one of the last things I expected to hear coming from my girlfriend's mouth, and it stopped me in my tracks. It was a good question, especially since we were in bed, where—after a hot and heavy round of foreplay—Julie was on her hands and knees with a pillow under her stomach that raised her ass up high. I'd been kneeling behind her, sawing away at her pussy, which was, as usual, dripping profusely; she really gushes when she's turned on. In fact, that's what triggered her query: she was so wet that my cock, which had been flying in and out of her like greased lightning, eventually slipped out, even though her entryway had been tightly constricted.

I'd repositioned my cockhead at her cunt in an attempt to

penetrate her again, but she was so slick that instead of piercing her vagina, I somehow managed to slide up her perineum. When I grazed her anus, her body gave a little jolt, like I'd hit some sort of hot button, one that I'd been unaware of up until that very moment. However, I didn't think anything of it until she piped up with that unexpected suggestion.

Anal sex was something I had thought about…a lot. However, I'd never given it a try because I hadn't thought my girlfriends, past or present, would be into it, but there was Julie, practically demanding that I put my cock in her butt. As I mused over this new possibility, I took hold of her cheeks and pulled them apart; that's when she looked back at me and smiled encouragingly, like she *really* wanted it. That erased any concern that she was doing it for my benefit alone, and even her rosebud seemed to be winking up at me as if to say, "Hey, you, c'mon in!"

I dipped a finger into her slippery cunt, and then, gently, I touched her pleated pink flesh and felt it pulse in response. I didn't see how my crown was going to fit in her back hole, much less the rest of my relatively thick shaft. Then I remembered back to a time when I was more inexperienced and thought the same thing about a woman's cunt. *Can't hurt to try*, I reasoned with myself and, thus emboldened, I massaged my girlfriend's asshole.

I was amazed by how quickly it reacted by relaxing a little and swallowing my fingertip. Julie moaned as the ring of muscle snapped shut around it and my imagination shot into overdrive. *How good would that feel around my dick?* I wondered, still incredulous that the opportunity to find out was so close at hand. That realization was hotter than all my fantasies put together, and I had to struggle not to get too carried away until my partner was also prepared. To achieve that end, I stroked her smooth canal from the inside, but it turned out that wasn't necessary. Obviously in no mood to dillydally, she shoved backward, impaling herself on my outstretched digit all the way to the bottom knuckle. "Just do it!" she exclaimed impatiently, and then she pulled away from my hand entirely, grabbed a nearby bottle of lube and tossed it in my direction.

My balls surged at the urgency in her voice, and I became as anxious as she was. Though I was tempted to shove right into her tight hole, there was something that I knew I had to do first. Squirting a generous dollop of lube into my palm, I jacked my shaft until it was glistening, and then slickened up her snug little hole. Julie wiggled impatiently, but I took my time to make sure we'd both be properly primed.

Satisfied that I was sufficiently lubed, I prepared myself for entry by grasping my cock at the base and positioning the crown at her nether hole. Julie continued her sexy undulations as she reared back toward me. Her eagerness made my balls ache.

With one hand on her hip, I tightened my grip with the other around the root of my dick to keep it steady. I pressed against her crimp, and then she moaned and leaned back onto me. I responded by applying more force and instantly felt her body working to accept me. I kept pressing forward, and when my cockhead popped through her aperture, we shared a labored sigh of both satisfaction and relief. Taking advantage of the momentum, I continued penetrating my girlfriend's rear canal, which swallowed the next few inches of my shaft easily. That's when I stopped to take a breath, overwhelmed by the snugness of that unfamiliar orifice.

Julie also seemed pleased by all the new sensations. Her body began to writhe, and I could hear her whimpering. However, I was so caught up in my own ardor that the sound seemed to be coming from miles away. I had to remind myself that she was right there in front of me, our bodies connected in a whole new way. Back in the here and now, I wanted to show her how much I appreciated her for making all this possible, so I wrapped my arms around her waist, pulled her closer, and placed soft kisses on her back and shoulders.

Still kissing my girlfriend's soft skin, I impaled her with the remainder of my length until her bottom cheeks came to rest on my balls. I stopped for a moment to take a breath, holding her tightly against me as I wondered if I could summon the strength to finish the job. Burrowing into Julie's ass hadn't depleted my energy; it was the emotional response that almost did me in. I felt like we'd taken our intimacy to a whole new level, and as we remained locked together for a few minutes more, my dick pulsed happily in its new home.

Julie's anus beat its own steady rhythm as it constricted and released my shaft, and the pace of that beat increased when I reached for her breasts to strum their lust-swollen tips. As she purred in response to my caresses, her body began writhing again, though her movements were almost imperceptible at first. Eventually, they grew more pronounced until her asshole was riding my rigid member. That much stimulation was way more than I could take; so much excitement coursed through my veins that I lost control.

Like a man possessed, I held on to Julie more tightly and yanked out my length until only the head was still wedged in her hole. She gasped as I pulled out and then she let out a grunt that was even louder when I sank back in. I was on autopilot, fucking her ass like I'd always fucked her cunt, but not without a few noticeable differences. This entryway felt hotter and closer, and it contracted around my cock much more tightly, creating an even snugger fit that didn't take much to get used to.

My girlfriend's reactions were different, too. Usually, she's very vocal, gasping and squealing and even talking dirty when I'm pounding into her. That night, however, she mostly remained quiet, although she would punctuate her silence with a grunt or growl whenever I shoved into her ass especially hard. From the way she squirmed, though, I knew that she was having as much fun as I was.

I didn't let go of my girlfriend's waist as I rocked my hips back and forth to repeatedly drive my length into her deepest regions. Over and over, I slammed against her asscheeks, while my sac slapped against her upper thighs. I knew it wouldn't be much longer before I climaxed.

Julie began to shake and shiver. She turned toward me, and when I caught a glimpse of her face, I saw that her features reflected that frustrating feeling of being so near climax that she could probably taste it. To tip her over, I leaned closer, placed my mouth at her ear and whispered hotly, "Go ahead, baby, touch yourself." She nodded, and then reached between her thighs to press her fingers to her clit. Although I couldn't see what she did after that, I felt her response, which came on fast and furious.

She reared up and then slammed back against me, swallowing my cock whole with the power of her movement. Seeing her take charge like that was so hot. As she came, still rubbing her sensitive button, her thighs clapped shut, trapping her hand between them.

I began jackhammering into her asshole, which pulsated rhythmically around me. I wanted to come before she finished climaxing, which I figured was a pretty good probability because she's usually multiorgasmic. As expected, she gave another huge shudder and muttered, "Oh yeah," and I gave her one last inward jab before I lost all semblance of control.

The next few minutes are a bit of a blur in my mind. My balls released their contents with explosive bursts rushing through my shaft and out the slit in my crown. My eruption lasted for what felt like an eternity. It was intense, to say the least, and my cock continued to throb between her asscheeks even after I'd delivered the last shot of my sticky seed. I'd never remained erect for that long after climaxing, and I even managed to give her a few more short strokes that supplied her with another small orgasm as her fingers danced over her clit. However, like all good things, this also had to end, and my dick finally softened, slipping from her delightful asshole.

After that night, anal sex became a regular occurrence for us, and it didn't take us long to discover that it was a two-way street. With any available orifice fair game for inquisitive fingers, Julie raised the stakes by trying to turn me on by tickling my asshole. Her actions worked, and it was soon as normal for her to pry apart my buttocks as it was for me to spread hers. Although it took a little getting used to, I quickly grew to love anal stimulation as much as she did, and we worked hard to figure out the easiest and most satisfying way for her to finger-fuck my tight chasm while I invaded hers with my dick. And once we invested in a few bottles of lubricant, nothing could slow us down.

Except, however, our being apart. Last week I was away on business for a few days, and by the time I got back into town, I was dying for a go at my girlfriend's behind. Turns out we were on the same wavelength because when I arrived at her apartment, she was waiting for me wearing nothing but a negligee and a big smile. The sheer black nightie stopped at the tops of her thighs, which gave me easy access to her butt and left me with absolutely no question about what she wanted—and how badly she wanted it.

As soon as the door closed behind us, she threw her arms around my neck, and I slid mine down to squeeze her luscious derriere. Our lips met, and I slipped my tongue into her mouth. Then, as I hoisted her up, she wrapped her legs around my waist, pressing her pussy against my burgeoning erection.

I carried her to the bedroom, never breaking our kiss, even when I leaned forward to gently deposit her on the mattress. She was so desperate for my dick that she immediately began scrabbling at my belt, so I sped things up by undressing myself. Then I flipped her negligee up over her tits, lay my body over hers, and slid my cock into her dripping-wet cunt.

I gave her a few good, hard strokes, already so worked up that I almost came too soon. I managed to catch myself in time and pulled out of Julie's pussy, albeit reluctantly. But that reluctance abated when I repositioned myself at her asshole and began nudging my way into it. My knob was so sticky with her copious juices that I slipped right in, and it also helped that she was used to such backdoor invasions. Her anus hugged my cockhead for a moment as though to welcome me home, but then it relaxed so I could follow through with the rest of my length.

I pulled out just as quickly, and she grabbed her bottle of lube. Pouring some into her palm, she slathered it onto my snug back hole, making sure her fingers got well greased in the process. Before tossing the bottle aside, she rubbed some lube into her own asshole. When I saw how ecstatic she looked massaging herself, I was beside myself with want. I nudged her hand away, and she bent back her legs until her knees practically touched her chest. Her labia peeled open enticingly, but I aimed a bit lower, at the crinkled rosebud that was the object of my lustful desire.

My ingress was once again easy, especially now that I was facilitated by the uber-slippery lube. As I slid past my girlfriend's anus, she bit down hard on her lower lip and squeezed her eyes shut. I loved being able to watch her face as I stroked in and out of her nether hole; she could never hide her emotions, and a satisfied smile was beginning to form. Then her expression grew mischievous, so I wasn't surprised when she reached around me to snake her hand between my bottom cheeks.

At first, only one slippery digit played with my anus, in order to relax it. Then she worked the tip inside, and I gasped as my balls drew in tight, ready to burst at the slightest provocation. She speared me to her bottom knuckle as I plunged in and out of her rear canal, which fluttered around my swollen shaft. She squirmed as she mimicked my steadily increasing pace with two outstretched fingers.

It felt like I had a slender cock pumping away inside me, and as a result, my own thrusts became deeper and more forceful. Again, she matched my rhythm as our movements became more frenzied. Usually, we take our time in order to draw out the pleasure for as long as possible, but since we hadn't seen each other in a while, we didn't even make an attempt to hold back our excitement.

Julie's mouth gaped open in what looked like a silent scream as she used her free hand to strum her clit and I repeatedly plunged into her. In return, she incessantly jammed her fingers into my asshole, which constricted more tightly around them as my excitement reached its peak. As she began thrashing wildly beneath me, her muscles snapped shut around my turgid shaft. No longer able to control her movements, she let her violent shivers do the rest of the work.

Watching my girlfriend come—as well as feeling her tremors vibrate throughout me—made my balls ready to explode. Rearing up, I shoved right back into her ass as a stream of semen ripped through my dick. She egged me on with both words and movements as I filled her to the brim with my load, which I continued pumping into her until there was nothing left to give. My cock kept throbbing for a few moments afterward, thanks to the soothing massage of her pulsating asshole, and as I slumped over onto her, I continued to enjoy the after-shocks of our shared orgasm. I was happy to be home from my trip, and even happier that my cock had found its own home in my girlfriend's willing—and welcoming—behind.

Anal Sex 101

JAKE DIXON

My girlfriend, Marnie, and I are graduate students at a West Coast university. We live in a small one-bedroom apartment just off campus, half a mile from the ocean. Barely a year removed from undergraduate work, Marnie is smart, attractive, and fun loving, with a real passion for life. Did I say attractive? Every inch of Marnie's five-foot-five, 115-pound body oozes sex appeal. She's got provocative green eyes, full red lips, and hair the color of dark chocolate. Weekends of sun and sea give her flawless skin a healthy bronze luster. Her breasts are a shade on the large side, yet perky and firm. Her flat stomach and curvy hips set off her sensational ass, which is exquisitely full and round. Our sex life has been great in the five months we've been together, but it really took off three weeks ago, when we made the discovery that Marnie loves anal sex. In fact, she absolutely craves it.

The first time was completely spontaneous—at least the anal part. It was a Thursday evening, and Thursdays are like Fridays for us because Marnie and I keep Fridays clear of classes and work. So we were in a weekend kind of mood that evening as we dined on pepperoni pizza and rum-and-Cokes. My girlfriend made a game of seeing how far she could stretch the cheese from her mouth, and before long she was a giggly mess, with mozzarella all over her fingers and chin. "I swear, Marnie," I said, laughing. "Sometimes I think you're twenty-two going on twelve." She just laughed harder and reached for another slice.

After we cleaned up (both the dishes and Marnie), she sidled up close to me and suggested we take a walk along the bluff that over-looks the ocean. My eyebrows rose—as well as my cock. Marnie likes to have sex in unusual or exotic places, so I had a feeling this walk would turn interesting. The previous Thursday, we had driven Marnie's old hatchback up into the hills and parked in a turnout to watch the sun set. I had barely turned off the ignition when Marnie twisted around to put the backseat down. What followed was a cramped but memo-rable romp in the back of the car, our naked bodies twisted like pret-zels against each other while Marnie's orgasmic cries drowned out the sound of passing cars.

So I agreed to the walk, and we headed out into the warm fall evening. Behind us, dusk was settling over the university campus, but the top of the clock tower still gleamed with orange light. Hand in hand, we followed the paved footpath as it wove along the cliff's edge. A hundred feet below, the Pacific crashed relentlessly ashore, its aqua-green breakers backlit by the setting sun. Marnie turned and led me off the path, picking her way through the tall brush. When we'd gone about fifty yards, she sank into the wild grasses and pulled me down beside her. We had encountered a few other people on the path, but now we were completely out of sight.

Flashing a beautiful, wanton grin at me, Marnie pulled her shorts and underwear completely off. She lay back on the ground and fingered her artfully groomed bush. I looked on as she spread her knees, displaying the wetness that coated the cleft of her smooth, hairless cunt lips. "See how hot I am for you, Jake?" she purred. "Come on, it's time for dessert."

My cock was at full mast as I crouched between her open thighs and pressed my face into her sex. No matter how many times I go down on Marnie, I am always thrilled by the plumpness of her labia. Marnie sighed with satisfaction and ran her fingers through my hair as I licked up and down her succulent folds.

When I came up for air a few minutes later, the sun was a giant red disk sitting right on the line where the sky met the sea. It was a beautiful sight, but not as beautiful as the opulence of Marnie's cunt and the puckered orifice just below, nestled in the crack of her perfect ass. Impulsively, I slid a finger into her sopping pussy, pulled it out and worked it into her anus. Marnie's sharp intake of breath made me stop a moment, but then she murmured, "That feels good!" I bent to lap at her clit while pushing my finger farther into her back hole, letting my saliva ease the way. Her sphincter tightened at first, but then it relaxed a notch and seemed to welcome my exploring digit. Beyond the opening, Marnie's rear channel was warm and yielding. Her pleasurable sighs got louder as my finger disappeared into her butt, all the way to the knuckle. "More," she purred. I saw a new excitement in her eyes, laced with desperation. I lubed another finger in her cunt and slipped it into her ass alongside the first one. Again, there was an initial resistance, followed by a perceptible relaxing. Marnie's sigh was long and passionate as she pulled her knees to her chest, thoroughly exposing herself. I added a third finger, carefully pushing through her clenching ring of muscle. "Oh, Jake," my girlfriend cried, tossing her head back and sweeping her hands through the surrounding brush.

I pulled my fingers partway out of her back channel, and then I pushed them back in again, pressing to the hilt. Marnie's rapturous cries fanned the flames of my own desire, and I began to wish it were my cock that was probing her ass. Marnie had the same idea, especially when I began pumping my fingers more aggressively into her butt. Her grunts and moans spurred me on. "That's it, that's it—oh fuck," she said with quiet intensity. She squirmed toward me in a frantic attempt to increase the sensation of fullness. "Use your cock, Jake," she urged. "I want to feel your fat dick in my ass."

I was as worked up as she was by this time, so I didn't hesitate to sit up, yank my pants down, and pull Marnie's ass into my lap. Breathing fast, I lined up my cock's stout head at her puckered opening and pushed gently forward—at least, I tried to. Despite the work of my fingers, it appeared that Marnie's tiny asshole might not be able to accommodate my prick. Undeterred, she sat up hastily, pressed my cock to her mouth, and slobbered furiously up and down the whole length of it. When she decided I was wet and slippery enough, the impatient girl lay back on the ground, but on her stomach this time, with the globes of her gorgeous ass lifted toward me. God, was she hot!

Licking my lips, I knelt between Marnie's thighs and replanted my erection at her anal opening. Then, with great care and persistence, accompanied by Marnie's breathy chants of "Yes, yes," I watched my glans disappear through her back door. It was an awesome sight, and an even more awesome feeling—so tight and warm, a velvety glove clutching my cock. Marnie took a deep breath as a wave of ecstasy rolled through her body, and then she exhaled, whispering unintelligibly. I did hear the word "intense," and when she looked back at me over her shoulder, the rapture in her face compelled me to keep pushing in deep. After about a minute, my entire prick was packed into her ass. Marnie went still for a moment, luxuriating in the sensation of being fully impaled. Then she began rocking forward and back, which propelled my cock in and out of her hole without any movement from me. For a second she seemed to swoon, so powerful were the feelings emanating from her rear. When I started to move again, driving my hard-on in and out of her ass, she came passionately alive. "You have no idea how incredible that feels," she hissed through clenched teeth. Her face was flushed and sweaty. I could feel her sphincter adjusting to the width and breadth of my advancing cock.

My excitement reached new levels, and I began to pump into Marnie's ass with quicker, more powerful thrusts. Distantly, I wondered whether the smutty sound of my balls slapping up against her skin could be heard from the nearby trail. The thought vanished as quickly as it had entered my mind, though, replaced by an all-consuming focus on Marnie's lush rear end. I could hardly believe the way her channel gripped my shaft from stem to stern, as if it were reluctant to ever let me go. My cock felt impossibly large in there.

I was soon on the brink of coming, but Marnie beat me to it. With a long, ecstatic cry that must have been heard by anyone passing by, my girlfriend gave in to a tempest of emotion. She scored the soft earth with her fingernails and thrust her ass up at me, forcing all of my erection inside her while the orgasm wracked her body. Seconds later, the spastic action of her anus spurred me to an equally violent climax. My cock pulsed between her buttocks as it shot a stream of warm cream into her deepest recesses. Marnie looked back at me, watching my face in the gathering darkness, vicariously enjoying my climax as hers finally began to ebb.

That was the first time. Three days later, I came to know beyond any doubt that Marnie was hooked on anal sex.

She called me on my cell phone from the campus library, where she works afternoons. "Can you come over here?" she asked, her voice sounding husky.

I looked around the kitchen, at the half-made dinner I had been preparing for the two of us. The digital clock on the microwave said it was almost six. "Shouldn't you be on your way home?"

"Not just yet, Jake. I need you here. Come, it'll be worth it."

"What's this about?"

"Just get over here. Please?"

She was scheming something naughty, I could tell. I didn't hesitate another second.

Walking fast through a surprisingly blustery and cool afternoon, I made my way across campus to the library. It's twelve stories high; you can see the ocean from the windows of the uppermost floors. The library closes early on Mondays, and students were coming out as I went in. Drifting toward the elevators, I whipped out my phone and punched in Marnie's number. "Where exactly are you?"

She giggled. "The ninth floor."

I kept the phone to my ear as I rode up. "Okay, now what?" I asked when the elevator doors opened.

"I'm way in back, on the left." She was keeping her voice down, but the note of desire was unmistakable. "The Human Sexuality section."

"Naturally," I said.

Walking by the windows, I looked out at the choppy sea and the deepening sky. Daylight still streamed in, but as I moved deeper among the stacks, the cool green tint of overhead fluorescents took over. The place was deserted except for Marnie, who I found between two of the many long rows of floor-to-ceiling bookshelves. She was sitting on the floor, surrounded by a dozen or more volumes that she'd pulled off the shelves—textbooks, illustrated guides, self-help manuals, even nude art books. I saw *The Atlas of Sexual Behavior, Legends of Human Sexuality,* and *Everything You Always Wanted to Know About Sex* (*But Were Afraid to Ask).* Many of the books lay open to passages and illustrations concerning anal sex. On one page, a table of statistics attempted to shed light on how many people were engaging in backdoor pleasures, and how often. I bent to pick up an especially eye-catching volume called *The Art of Sexual Ecstasy,* which was open to a highly detailed pencil drawing of a woman sitting astride a man with his cock buried in her ass. My pulse was racing, and my dick was hardening up fast. Marnie's gaze locked with mine, and I saw how worked up she was. She had been researching her new passion all afternoon, fanning the flames of her desire at the same time. A slight movement caught my attention: she had her hand shoved down her panties, working feverishly at her cunt.

"They're locking up downstairs," I said, feeling my dick throb.

Marnie grinned. "I work here, remember? My key will get us out." She pulled off her shirt, revealing a black bra beautifully filled out by her fulsome breasts. She unbuttoned her skirt next, but she left it halfway down her hips in her impatience to get at my fly. I staggered back against the bookshelves as she worked my jeans and underwear down to my knees. Taking hold of my manhood, Marnie knelt before me and rubbed the glans over her face, leaving a trace of precome on her chin. Then she closed her lips around my rod and began to suck me. Relaxing her throat, she bobbed up and down with an eagerness that made her dark hair sway wildly about her shoulders. Holding on to the books nearest me, I swayed my hips back and forth, watching as my cock slid in and out of Marnie's sensual lips. The library was perfectly silent now, except for the sound of Marnie gorging herself on my penis. I felt a thrill at the incongruence of our surroundings.

Stopping to catch her breath, Marnie said, "You taste so good, Jake." She flicked her tongue across my cock's oozing slit, then licked along the underside of my staff and began lapping at my balls. Still pumping my dick with her hand, she suckled on my ball sac with an unquenchable appetite. I wasn't sure how much more I could take, but Marnie gave me a reprieve when she stopped briefly to pull my jeans and underwear completely off. Crawling farther back between my legs, she surprised me by pressing her face to my ass. Then, with great enthusiasm, she snaked her tongue between my buttocks to lick my perineum and my rear hole. My yelp of astonishment quickly turned into a moan of sheer delight as I relaxed into the delicious feeling. She was still reaching around to stroke my cock, which was more turgid than ever.

Eager for more, I spread my feet wider on the floor to give Marnie better access to my hole. I felt her lips press against my back door, and then she began to rim me avidly, making noisy slurping sounds that whipped up my excitement to an almost unbearable level.

I shuddered, gripping the bookshelves, when her inquisitive tongue slipped inside my anus. The tip fluttered inside me, probing, and I came unglued. Gobs of come squirted from my cock as I experienced one of the most intense orgasms of my life. Marnie's hand flew up and down my rod, and she continued to lap at my hole until I was spent.

The incorrigible girl wanted me to return the favor, which I was only too eager to do. Marnie scooted out from between my legs and stripped off her skirt and panties, which were soaked with her juices. Her green eyes shone brightly with passion as she lay back on the floor and held her asscheeks apart, showing me her now-favorite erogenous zone. I got down there and gave her the same treatment she'd given me, licking her little orifice with gusto. She wiggled around, relishing the feel of my tongue on her sensitive opening.

After a few minutes, I sensed she was anxious to experience deeper, more intense sensations back there, so I turned over to lie flat on my back, and Marnie quickly mounted me, settling her beautiful haunches onto my thighs. Taking hold of my monster prick, which had retained its steely hardness, she saw that it was still dripping a few last drops of come. With a delighted giggle, she bent and licked the whole crown clean. Then she grabbed a tube from her bag and lubed me up before she lifted herself up, her shapely thighs flexing, and held my prick to her eager anus. The sight of her rapturous face as she began to slide incrementally down my pole was as exquisite as the feel of her squeezing hole. Farther and farther down she went, her mouth forming a small, tense circle, until she reached the bottom of my lengthy spike. It wasn't only the tightness of her sphincter that felt so amazing, but also the way her full, round asscheeks clung to my shaft as it slid between them.

Marnie's dark hair partly hid her face as she sat impaled for a moment, assimilating my cock in her back channel. Then she raised herself six or seven inches, keeping only the tip inside, before easing down once more. Her luscious buttocks enveloped my prick the whole way. She tossed her hair out of her eyes and looked deep into my own as she lifted and lowered, taking me slowly but surely into the farthest reaches of her ass. She picked up the pace as she acclimated to the presence of my thick intruder in her anal passage. Soon she was riding me briskly, her cries of pleasure coming in a rapid staccato.

A faraway look came into Marnie's eyes as she eventually hit her stride. I felt her thighs tighten, and she sat up straighter on my swollen cock, tangling her hands in her hair. I liked her best like that, vigorously bouncing up and down on me with her arms raised, like a bull rider who disdains the saddle's horn. I was so deep in the warm glove of her ass that I could hardly stand it. I reached for the front clasp of her bra and yanked it open, freeing her gorgeous breasts. She settled firmly onto my root and ground her asshole in a circular motion against the base of my cock, which also mashed her distended clit against my pelvis. Her eyes fluttered closed and her whole body stiffened, just as I felt the first kick of orgasm deep in my dick. A moment later, Marnie lost all control. Her body shuddered powerfully, but she could only whimper as the explosion of indescribable pleasure ripped through her. I felt her asshole flexing around my prick, milking me. With a final grunt of satisfaction, I emptied my balls into Marnie's back channel, glazing her deepest passage with hot cream. She was almost sobbing with joy by now, her body lying prone atop me while her ass coaxed out every last drop of my semen. At last I felt my cock begin to soften, but Marnie didn't move; she just held on to me, happy to keep my dick inside her well-worked butt for as long as she possibly could.

We snuck out of the dimly lit library a little while later, using a back door on the bottom floor to make our escape. Marnie was sated for the time being, but that was temporary. We had awakened a new fire in her, a new obsession—one that I am happy to continue helping her explore.

Cycle of Lust

WARREN SHULMAN

When it comes to bicycling, there are casual riders, there are enthusiasts, and then there's Terri, my girlfriend, a cycling fanatic. Not only does she love bicycling as a sport, she's also into her bike as a practical matter, using it whenever possible to go where she wants to go. Every day she pedals to and from her job, which is nine miles from our house. On weekends, rain or shine, she goes for early morning rides into the countryside and returns hours later, beaming and covered in sweat.

Don't misunderstand me; Terri's not a fitness fiend. It's just bicycling she loves, and all that riding has given her twenty-six-year-old body a beautifully toned and supple shapeliness—especially her hips, legs, and ass. She turns heads wherever we go. With flowing red hair and a strikingly beautiful face to go along with that bicycling-sculpted body, Terri's pretty amazing. I especially like her butt, which has to be the most delectable rear end I have ever had the pleasure to behold—or to fuck. You see, the only thing Terri likes more than riding her bike is riding my cock when it's deep in her ass. Her passion for both activities led me to join her recently in an annual charity ride up a local mountain road, which in turn led to our most memorable anal sex session ever.

Terri participates in the event every year, joining more than a hundred bicyclists in the challenge of pedaling to a mountain summit at the edge of town. The pine forest at the top is almost 7,000 feet above sea level, and some riders quit before they get there, but Terri always makes it. I admire her dedication to the sport and her interest in helping a good cause, but I am nowhere near the cycling devotee that she is. Still, I agreed this year to ride the last part of the route with her. First, however, I was going to volunteer a couple of hours at one of the water station checkpoints alongside the road.

The ride started at sunrise, which meant we had to get up before dawn. Terri was wide-awake and excited as we ate breakfast, but all I felt like doing was going back to bed. I'm not a morning person. As we cleared our plates, I found myself expressing misgivings. "I'm not sure about this," I said, yawning. "My bike's pretty old…"

I wasn't really going to back out and Terri knew it, but she pretended that I needed encouragement. "Don't get cold feet now," she said, sidling up to me with bright, eager eyes. Her tank top and spandex bike shorts looked like they were painted onto her tight, luscious body. "I want you with me this time, Warren. It wouldn't be as much fun without you."

"I don't know," I persisted, playing along. "Maybe I could just wait for you here."

"You could," Terri purred coyly, "but then you'd miss out on all the fun we're going to have at the top, after we cross the finish line. *Private* fun." Her hands were on my shoulders, her face turned up to mine, and in her eyes I saw the special twinkle she gets whenever she's feeling especially horny. My cock stirred rapidly to life, forming an uncomfortable bulge in my shorts. Terri's crotch was inches from my hand. I touched her there, stroking the shiny material stretched tautly across her pussy. She trembled slightly, then more noticeably as I curved my hand around her sex. I could feel the heat of her desire emanating from her cunt. She shivered against me when I ran my thumb across the approximate spot where her clit was. She turned around so that my hand was in the crack of her sexy ass.

"Why wait until the finish?" My voice was thick with desire as I nuzzled Terri's neck and ran my hands over her breasts. "Of course, we might be late..."

"Then let's be late," my wanton girlfriend said. Turning and fixing me with her lusty grin, she peeled off her bicycling outfit in record time. I got naked, too, and we stumbled to the nearest chair. Terri had me sit down, and then she knelt before me on the kitchen floor. My cock looked obscenely large and thick as it swayed in front of her pretty face. She curled her fingers around the base and began licking hungrily up and down the shaft. Soon my whole prick was wet and shiny. Brushing a lock of her red hair out of her face, Terri made a wide-open circle with her lips and started to swallow me. She got half my length into her mouth, then eased back and bobbed forward again, swallowing more. I watched as her pink lips slid back and forth with increasing speed over my staff. Terri has always been good at giving head, and this time was no exception. Her tongue swirled expertly around my dick, agitating my sensitive glans and bringing me dangerously close to creaming down her throat.

Neither of us wanted me to come yet, though, so after enjoying another minute of her oral attentions, I stopped my voracious girl. "Kneel on the chair," I suggested, but Terri was already assuming that position, since it's one of her favorites for anal penetration. She held on to the chair back and stuck her ass out, so that the cheeks of her gorgeous rear end swelled out toward me, creamy smooth and begging to be fucked. Just below her tiny asshole, the pink petals of her cunt gleamed with a copious flow of her natural lubricant. Terri maintains a narrow strip of russet-colored pubic hair above her slit, but viewed from the rear, as I saw her now, her pussy looked completely clean shaven. I ran my hand through her silky-wet folds, carefully working her up into an even greater state of arousal. Then I bent and slipped my tongue between her thickened labia to get a taste of her juices. She was so wet; I had a mouthful of her tangy honey in seconds. Terry spread her knees wider in the chair, and I felt her fingers join my tongue at her slit. "Do me, Warren," she cried as she plied her cunt. "I need to feel you in my ass." She reached farther back between her legs and rubbed her sticky fingers around the rim of her anus. As I watched, she pushed her index finger into the puckered hole. "Please," she urged, practically whimpering, "push your cock into my ass *now*."

I stood behind her and prepared to plunder her curvy behind. Terri looked back at me over her shoulder and pushed her butt out farther, which opened the cleft a little more. I slotted my throbbing cock between those plush cheeks and pressed gently against her tight back door. My cock, rock hard and thicker than ever, was still well lubed from Terri's sloppy oral attentions, and I popped through her pliant hole relatively easily. "Mmm, yes," she breathed as the bulbous glans at the top of my shaft worked its way up her back channel. "Yes, that's it…" Her words trailed off as the sensation of fullness momentarily overwhelmed her, and then, adjusting, she began to push back onto my pole, impaling herself. Finding her voice again, she exclaimed, "Oh my god!" Her kneeling body undulated in the chair, awash with pleasure, and her auburn hair flounced against her pale back. I had only to hold on to her warm hips, lean into her and let her take me, inch by inch, into the deepest recesses of her ass. The incredible tightness and heat sent powerful tingles through my prick and down into my balls.

We established a nice rhythm as I began pumping more freely into her welcoming behind. Terri's impending three-hour ride atop her bicycle seat was in both our minds, so our tempo was more measured than usual, but no less deep or intense. Terri kept one hand at her cunt, where she alternated between rubbing her engorged clit and pumping her fingers in and out of her dripping hole. I filled my hands with her generous breasts and rolled the nipples between my fingers. All the while, I kept sinking my dick into Terri's fanny, withdrawing a few inches and plunging in again, always to the hilt. My balls slapped against her buttocks with a loud, sticky sound in the otherwise quiet kitchen. The shades covering the kitchen windows were just beginning to glow with dawn's early light when I felt that delicious kick at the base of my cock. I grunted and bucked into my girlfriend's ass a final time, burying my staff completely. Terri's feral howl of delight accompanied the surge of semen from my balls. As I filled her ass with hot cream, she came unglued, writhing in the chair with such emotion that I feared we would both topple to the floor.

Soon we both came back to our senses, and there was no time to waste. I threw her a towel to tidy up, and then we hurried into our clothes and raced into the garage, where our bikes and helmets were already in the back of the pickup truck.

Luck was with us, and Terri wasn't late, after all. At the starting line, she wended her way through the crowd of bicyclists and checked in with the event organizers. Then she tied her hair back and donned her helmet. I brought her bike over. "See you in a couple of hours," I said. She kissed me passionately and whispered in my ear, "Your cream is still trickling out of me." Her words caused my cock to throb back to life. *Later*, I told myself. I gave her ass a parting squeeze, then got back in my truck and headed up the mountain.

After several miles, I spotted the checkpoint where I'd be spending most of the morning. I parked well off the shoulder and joined other volunteers who were setting up a bicycle repair station and refreshment table. The morning was well advanced when the first riders began to show up. Terri came along soon after, glistening with sweat and breathing hard. "Not far to go now," she said. "You ready?"

"Ready as I'll ever be," I replied, handing her a cup of water.

"Don't forget the private fun I promised," Terri whispered, and she emphasized the thought with a sensual kiss.

I got my bike out of the truck, and soon we were pedaling alongside each other on our way up to the summit. It took us over an hour to get there, during which I gained new respect for Terri's physical and mental toughness.

We reached the finish line around noon. The mountain air was cool and fresh compared to the stifling triple-digit heat down in the city. My thighs burned and my lungs ached, but I felt a sense of exhilaration. We milled around with other riders for a while as we refueled with drinks and snacks. Then we got back on our bikes and followed a trail into the woods, leaving the crowd behind. Terri and I had gone hiking up here before, so we knew where to go to lose ourselves in the forest. The tall pines swayed gently in the breeze, their whisper a seductive invitation to stay and play.

After a half hour's ride, the trail skirted a magnificent clearing. We stopped and watched the wind create waves in the straw-colored grass. Terri dismounted her bike and started walking. I hurried after her. Behind me, the long grass quickly rebounded, obscuring our passage. When we reached what was more or less the center of the expanse, it felt like we had the whole world to ourselves. All was quiet except for the sound of the breeze rustling through the grass and the forest beyond. Terri traipsed around making patterns underfoot, her long hair shining fiery red in the strong sunlight. "This is perfect," she said, grinning at me.

"For what?"

"You know what." Her glance dropped to the obvious hard-on in my shorts, and her voice was bold and saucy as she said, "I want you to fuck my ass right here, Warren." She was already pulling her tank top over her head, exposing her gorgeous tits to the sun. Next, with complete unconcern, she peeled off her sweat-soaked bike shorts and panties and dropped them both to the grass. Naked now, except for her cross-trainers and socks, Terri stood there, flaunting her incredibly fine body for the world to see. But there were only the birds, the trees, and me. She saw the look in my eyes, and her own expression became infused with lust. I started taking off my clothes, and she hurried over to help me.

Once nude, I sank onto the grass and pulled Terri down beside me. I was as eager to bury my throbbing cock into her rear channel as she was to take me there, but I wanted to draw out the anticipation. Terri loves the feel of my mouth on her cunt and on her smaller, tighter hole, and I wasn't going to disappoint her.

Easing her down onto her back, I sat on my heels for a moment and absorbed the sight of her feminine beauty. The high-altitude light bathed Terri's body with an ivory brilliance that perfectly illuminated her many assets, from her heaving breasts to her flat belly and her smooth cunt. She drew up her knees, exposing the fleshiest part of her asscheeks. I looked on as she ran her hand over her pussy, tracing her fingertips through her dewy labia and across the narrow strip of pubic hair. When she withdrew her fingers, those tangerine-colored curls gleamed wetly.

"Stop grinning and eat me," Terri pleaded, holding her other hand to her eyes to shield them from the bright sunlight. I lowered my head to her exquisite crotch and inhaled her feminine musk. When I pressed the tip of my tongue into her dripping folds, she sighed dreamily. Terri's honey was sweetly pungent after the morning's strenuous exercise. I lapped up those heady juices with a fervor that made my lover squirm in the grass. She was really sopping by now, and hot—both literally and figuratively. I focused my attentions on her sensitive clit, teasing her with my lips and breath. She drew her fingers through my hair, tugging it and urging me on. I darted my tongue into her velvety pussy, then returned to her clitoral nub, spreading her juices all over the place. She clamped her supple thighs to the sides of my face but eased off a bit when she sensed I was ready to move lower, where she wanted me most. Snaking my tongue along her sun-kissed skin, I delved into the crack of her ass. "Oh, yes," Terri murmured. I held the fleshy cheeks apart and observed her anus at close range. My own desire flared anew as I rimmed that puckered hole and then slipped my tongue inside. My limber lover bucked and squirmed in the grass and encouraged me with a string of excited yelps. While I continued to tongue Terri's asshole, I reached for her enlarged clit, which was just above my nose. I rolled that swollen button beneath my thumb, making Terri writhe around like a woman possessed. A few seconds later, she came hard against my mouth with a shout. It was a brief but intense climax that left her momentarily breathless.

Moving quickly, I rose up to my knees and slid my prick into Terri's still-quivering cunt, missionary-style. A few thrusts to the hilt were all I needed to thoroughly coat my rod with her juice. Then I withdrew and aimed myself at Terri's anus like it was a bull's-eye. She pulled her knees toward her chest, reached under her butt and held herself wide open, offering me her well-swabbed opening. I nudged my cockhead against her sphincter and then pushed right through it, feeling the ring of muscle seal up around my shaft. Beyond that tight aperture, Terri's silky channel felt bottomless.

A sudden gust of wind swept over and around us, momentarily cooling our sweaty bodies. Terri clawed at my ass, trying to pull me in deeper.

"I've been dreaming about this for weeks," she muttered passionately. "Your cock filling me up back there, under a blue sky..." Her voice trailed off into a series of grunts as I eased my prick farther into her ass. Her pussy overflowed with juices that seeped down to ease my way. Despite my own carnal desire to plunge in hard and quick, I was sensitive to the fact that Terri might be sore from the long, difficult bike ride. But she dispelled those notions immediately. "I'm fine," she assured me between excited gasps. "Fuck me hard, Warren!" She showed she was serious by bucking up at me, which drove my dick deep into her anal core. She moaned with animalistic fervor, threw her head back and shoved again, stuffing her ass full of my cock.

With that kind of encouragement, I let myself go. Terri's exceptional derriere took my powerful thrusts with aplomb. I crammed my whole length all the way in, then pulled out a little before plowing back in to the root. I could feel her sphincter flex, a sublime clenching and releasing against my cock as I sawed back and forth through her gripping orifice.

Feeling a huge climax approaching, I withdrew from Terri's well-worked ass and she turned over onto her stomach to enjoy our carnal finale from the rear. As I crouched over her, she lifted her flushed buttocks to meet me, and my cock practically slid back into her ass by itself. As I reseated my hard-on wholly in her behind, Terri asked in a voice hoarse with lust, "How do you like your reward for undertaking such a long, hard ride?"

"Baby, I'd pedal up Mount Everest for this," I said between gasps as I pounded into her heavenly tush a few final times. Then I was unable to speak any further as the sensation of Terri's inner anal walls tightening against my shaft made me lose control. Hot semen spat from my penis like machine-gun fire into the farthest reaches of her ass. Just like before, my climax sent Terri into an orgasmic fit. She undulated beneath me, smashing down the grass with her thrashing body as the wind carried off her cries of ecstasy. When I finally pulled out of her clutching anus, my cock dribbled a few last drops of come onto her asscheeks. Terri reached back and rubbed the cream into her skin as at last she, too, began to calm down.

Later, we enjoyed the exhilarating experience of coasting down the mountain at breakneck speed as the sun set. Since that wonderful adventure, I've become as enthusiastic about bicycling events as she is, because the rides always end like they did that day—with exciting anal encounters we will never forget.

Winning Team

Jack Dawson

The candidate wasn't expected to take the podium until eight o'clock, but by six the hotel ballroom was standing room only. I drove two hours to join the rally; it's not every day you get to be in the same room with someone who may be the next leader of the free world. So I stood shoulder to shoulder with hundreds of strangers while a live band kept everyone pumped up. I hardly expected to meet someone like Annie, who was about to turn my mind (and body) completely away from politics.

At first she was just a stranger standing next to me, part of the loud, enthusiastic crowd. Then I felt a touch on my arm. "Great turnout, huh?" the girl shouted over the din.

Realizing someone had addressed me, I turned and nodded in the direction of the voice. "Hope the fire marshal doesn't get wind of this."

To be honest, she wasn't the type who typically catches my eye. She was of average height and slender, with modest curves and short black hair that matched her eyeglass frames. She was in her late twenties, thirty at most, whereas I was pushing forty. Her blue jeans, well worn and faded, sat low on her waist and her T-shirt bore a popular political slogan. I caught her studying me as I was studying her, and I noticed that her brown eyes were bright and intelligent. Something in her look sent a throb of desire coursing through my cock.

"Did you see the debate last week?" she asked. We talked about that for a while, then about other aspects of the campaign. She introduced herself, and we learned a lot about each other as we waited for the overdue candidate. Annie had an engaging personality. Like me, she was an active volunteer for the campaign. We had the same ideas, and we cared about the same issues. I admired her passion as she spoke about her views of the world. I also began to see that she was not without physical charms—in fact, she was quite attractive, much more so than I'd initially thought. She had a cute smile and showed it often, her pretty face lighting up in a way I found beguiling.

At one point the crowd jostled us, and I felt Annie's high, firm breasts brush against my arm. I couldn't help glancing at her chest; her nipples were pointy and stiff beneath her thin cotton T-shirt. She caught my look and glanced down at herself. "Pretty cold in here," she joked, and we both laughed, since the opposite was true. Annie was slightly in front of me when she turned to applaud the musicians onstage, and that's when I noticed her tight, perky ass. I'm a connoisseur of that particular part of the female anatomy, and Annie's butt was gorgeous. She wore her jeans low enough to provide an occasional glimpse of her blue thong and a little butterfly tattoo at the small of her back. My first impressions had been turned upside down: Annie was hot. Fortunately, it was pretty obvious that the attraction was mutual—Annie was in full flirting mode.

The sexual tension between us was well advanced when, two hours later, the man we'd all been waiting for finally walked onto the stage. The crowd cheered heartily and then fell silent as his speech began. Annie positioned herself in front of me and leaned back a little. I felt her ass against my groin and smelled the floral scent of her hair. I rested my hands on her lissome hips and made sure she could feel my huge hard-on. She rubbed her beautiful rear end against me in response, making my breath quicken.

When the speech was over, Annie cheered as loudly as anyone in the room. Her youthful enthusiasm was intoxicating.

Turning to me, she said, "The bar looked pretty cool. Join me for a drink?"

"Sure."

I followed her out of the ballroom and across the opulent lobby to the hotel bar. I ordered a vodka tonic, prompting a surprised look from Annie. "My favorite. I'll have the same," she told the bartender.

It was that kind of night. Sparks continued to fly as our conversation became more intimate. Annie, who had booked a room at the hotel, ordered a second round of drinks. When I offered a halfhearted protest, citing my long drive home, she smiled coyly. "You can't go now, Jack. Besides, the night is young."

Technically, it wasn't—it was after midnight. "I like the way you think," I said, clinking my glass with hers. "In fact, I've never had so much in common with anyone as I do with you. Is it possible for two people to agree on everything?"

"I don't know," she said, her smile full of mirth. "Let's test this. Baseball or football?"

"Baseball," I said.

"Yep. Favorite music?"

"Eighties rock," I replied. "You?"

"Country-western," she said. "There, a disagreement!" We both laughed. Annie took a sip from her drink and forged onward. "Okay. Favorite sexual position?" My pulse quickened. She grinned and added, "Come on, Jack. I'll tell you mine if you tell me yours."

"Okay," I replied. "Go ahead."

She smiled wider. "I like them all."

"I like them all, too. Be specific."

She ran a finger around the rim of her glass. "It's not the position that matters," she said, "it's where you put it."

I shifted in my seat, trying to make my erection less uncomfortable as I realized what she meant. Annie laughed and poured the last of her drink down her throat. Then she set the empty tumbler on the bar, leaned in close to me and whispered, "Come up to my room and I'll be more specific."

"Check, please," I called out hoarsely to the bartender.

Annie's room was on the ninth floor. The door clicked shut behind us, and I pulled her to me. Annie's hunger was as fierce as my own. Just breaking away to flip on the light took a supreme effort of will. Her tongue explored my mouth aggressively while her hands made quick work of my belt buckle and zipper. She paused to pull her T-shirt off, revealing her modestly sized, perfectly shaped breasts and the dusting of freckles between them. I reached out to caress those adorable mounds, enjoying their warmth and firmness. The small pink nipples stood stiffly at attention, and I tweaked them between my fingers, making Annie gasp with pleasure. She mashed her lips to mine while pressing the whole length of her lithe body against me.

"You were saying in the bar…" I prompted her.

Annie giggled and pulled me, stumbling, toward the bed. "First things first," she said. Dropping onto the mattress, she kicked off her shoes and held her feet up so I could tug off her jeans. Then, clad in nothing but her thong underwear and a promiscuous smile, she crawled to me and pulled my pants and boxers down to my ankles. My fully erect cock swayed out, and she grabbed hold of it. Without a moment's delay, she took my helmet-shaped glans into her mouth, followed by most of the shaft. I stood beside the bed and leaned gently into her, feeling my tool slide along her tongue. She moaned deep in her throat, a moan that registered as exquisite vibrations along the length of my rod. Using her free hand, she manipulated my ball sac with a sensual, almost reverential touch. Her mouth felt like a soft, pliant cave around my cock as she bobbed back and forth. She was going to coax the semen right out of my balls if I let her go on much longer.

Annie sensed the level of my arousal and let me go in time. My prick swung free, totally greased with her saliva. Turning around on her hands and knees, she wagged her luscious fanny at me. Her eyes burned with need as she looked back over her shoulder and declared, "The truth is, the only thing that gets me going more than politics is a big, hard dick in my ass."

"Then we're both in luck," I said, whipping off my shirt and shedding a couple of buttons in the process. Kneeling behind her on the bed, I grabbed the thin strip of fabric that ran between her asscheeks and pulled it aside. As I did so, my fingers brushed against her dripping pussy. I couldn't resist the urge to bend down and snake my tongue into her soft, velvety folds. Annie's cunt tasted heavenly, and I kept licking her for another minute or two, enjoying the tickle of her wiry pubic hair against my lips. She shuddered with pleasure, but I knew she was desperate for anal play, so I straightened up at last.

Using my fingers, I spread her copious pussy juices up into the groove of her ass, lubricating her anus. Her thong started to slip back between those creamy orbs and Annie reached for the garment with annoyance. "Rip it off," she commanded me, so I jerked the thin fabric hard between my fists and it came away with a satisfying snap. Dropping the bits of cloth on the floor, I aimed my quivering dick at the enticing bull's-eye between her buttocks.

"You never told me your favorite position," Annie said breathlessly as I pressed my dick against her back door.

"This is it," I said, as my cockhead popped through her sphincter. Annie gasped and held still for a moment, then pushed back at me. I squeezed her smooth asscheeks in my hands and watched her cleaving hole swallow my dick. She was amazingly tight yet supple back there, and it felt so good that I wanted to push inside without delay. Somehow I managed to restrain myself and let Annie set the pace. She continued to push back with insistent pressure, sighing with gratification as her narrow channel yielded to the passage of my cock. When her ass was pressed up against my groin, she pulled her knees forward a little more, which forced the last half inch of my shaft into her bottom. Then she began to rock against me, panting with intense pleasure. Most of my penis stayed hidden in her ass, where the sensitive knob bored into her deepest recesses.

I started moving with Annie, timing my thrusts to meet her

sweet body each time she rocked back at me. The feeling was incredible, and soon we were both moaning like animals in heat. Incensed with passion, she pitched back and forth on her hands and knees, ramming against me with total abandon. Feeding off her enthusiasm, I pumped away at her ass, watching my thick shaft stretch her tiny hole to the limit. "Oh, oh, oh!" Annie moaned, and then her voice became a cry of joy as she exclaimed, "I'm coming!" She dropped her face and shoulders to the mattress, muffling her sobs of ecstasy. Her hands twisted the sheets into knots, and her whole body trembled with the force of her climax. I kept on jacking into her delectable ass, feeling more revved up than ever. A moment later I felt a kick at the root of my cock as the cream rose swiftly from my balls. Holding on to her shoulders, I pumped deeply into her behind one last time and then cut loose, glazing her back channel with a full load of come. That sent Annie into a series of orgasmic aftershocks that were almost as powerful as her initial climax. She was an amazingly passionate girl.

She dropped flat to the bed, and I rolled onto the mattress beside her. Within minutes, we were both asleep. I slept like a rock for about six hours, and when I awoke, the room was filled with morning light. Annie had just opened the drapes. She stood at the window looking out, her hair wildly mussed. She had nothing on but my shirt, which barely concealed her essentials.

"Good morning," I said.

She turned, smiled, and came to me for a kiss. "How about breakfast?" she asked, picking up the phone beside the bed. I nodded, so she called room service, and I hopped in the shower. About twenty minutes later, there was a knock at the door, and Annie went to answer it. Watching the movement of her perky ass, my mind was filled with the memory of our fuckfest the night before. Just thinking about it stirred my cock to life.

Annie came back with a tray laden with food. I sat on the bed, and she sprawled on her stomach beside me, my shirt riding up over her haunches. The food was good, but I found myself distracted by Annie's exposed ass. I rested one hand at the top of her thigh where it met her buttock. Her skin there was ultrasoft and satiny. She munched on a sausage and giggled as I slid my hand up over the swell of her ass. When I reached between her willowy thighs to touch her sex, she moaned a little, lifting her hips to give me better access. I massaged her vulva softly, barely touching her clit, which was enough to send tremors of pleasure rippling through her frame. Somehow we both kept eating our meal, but by the time our stomachs were satisfied, our sexual appetites were fully aroused.

"Let's get rid of this," I said, moving the empty tray from the bed to the night table. When I turned back to Annie, she reached toward me to remove my shirt. Afterward, I watched her roll onto her side, nude, and I felt a surging pulse in my groin. Annie lifted one knee high, giving me a good look at her sex in the bright light of morning. The triangle of pubic hair was thick and black, tapering into a carefully manicured point just above her vulva. Feeling my breath come quickly, I stretched out next to Annie in a side-by-side sixty-nine and pressed my face into her pretty pussy. She was already reaching for my cock, which was fully erect and desperate for action. I felt her lips close over my shaft and her tongue swirl around the glans. She sucked at my rod with such diligence and verve that I had a hard time concentrating on her cunt. I couldn't see what she was doing down there, but it felt like she was taking my whole length into her throat. I darted my tongue into her sopping folds and lapped at her swollen clit. Now it was Annie's turn to be distracted. She cried out and jerked her hips toward me, but to her credit, she kept my cock firmly between her lips. Her hot button seemed to swell even larger as I flicked it back and forth, and before long, I had Annie right on the edge of coming.

"Let me feel you inside me," she exclaimed, letting go of my rigid shaft. She lay on her back and opened her legs wide, an eager supplicant for my cock. Her face was flushed, and her sex glistened with need. Scrambling into position, I leaned above her on my hands and felt my dick nudge the cleft of her pussy. Her ass was the ultimate goal for both of us, but I wanted to draw out the anticipation. Gently splitting her labia with my dick, I felt the walls of her cunt ripple against my shaft, coaxing me in. Annie's eyelids drooped, and she sighed dreamily as I pushed fully inside her sopping depths. "That feels wonderful, Jack," she moaned.

I smiled and leaned low to kiss her while I began to saw in and out of her cunt. She dug her fingers into my ass and squeezed my glutes in time with my thrusts. I nipped her lovely neck and fucked her faster, making her gasp. She let go of my butt with one hand, wet a finger in her mouth and reached down to stimulate her favorite hole. "Oh, yes," she stammered, gazing at me through slitted eyes. Then, flashing a naughty grin, she brought her other hand to her mouth, wet a finger and reached for my ass. The touch of her eager finger on my anus made me cry out. It was so good and so unexpected that I almost shot my wad right then. She continued to stimulate my tiny hole, and hers, as I powered my cock in and out of her pussy. "I need you in my ass now," she pleaded passionately. "Come on, Jack, stuff my butt with your fat prick."

I pulled out of her juicy cunt, and Annie pulled her knees to her chest, opening the groove of her ass wide. I couldn't help licking my lips. She watched from between her knees as I prepared to push into her rosebud. My cock, thoroughly lubed with her natural honey, prodded her springy hole and then slid inside. Annie let out a long, wolfish moan, and I felt her channel begin to relax. When I was halfway in, I paused to savor the way her dilating sphincter clutched my penis. Annie moved her hips a little, urging me onward, so I leaned into her again and watched as the rest of my fully distended cock crammed inside her back passage. Once I was completely wedged in there, I waited a beat and then started driving in and out with the kind of force I knew she craved. She started tossing her head on the pillow and lifting her hips to meet my thrusts. I locked my arms straight and really let go, slamming into her ass at full tilt. The flexible girl hooked her ankles over my shoulders, which drove me even deeper into her butt.

Her back hole repeatedly clenched and released my organ in rapid-fire pulses of ecstasy. A swell of incredible sensation welled up inside me and blasted through my entire body. Grunting like a madman, I plowed into Annie's beautiful ass a final time, pulled out at the last second, and shot my creamy load all over her trembling breasts. Exhausted, I fell onto the bed beside her. She turned onto her side and threw her arms around me; we stayed like that for a long time.

Later, after taking a shower together, we made plans to meet again at the candidate's next big rally, which would be held in a neighboring state. Frankly, I didn't care how far I had to travel to see Annie again. Luckily for me, she felt exactly the same way.

Stacia's Surprise

CHARLIE REYNOLDS

I couldn't stop staring at her ass. It was a perfect specimen, round and tight, encased in a pair of those skinny-leg jeans that all the girls are wearing these days. Undressing her with my eyes, I peeled off the form-fitting pants and then hooked my fingers under the waistband of the thong that I was certain would be underneath. Her gorgeous buttocks would then be revealed, two globes of supple flesh that begged me to sink my erection between them. As I pictured myself pulling my cock back out, I could practically feel my balls pulse.

"Honey, what are you staring at?" Guiltily, I looked up from my seat at the kitchen table, the remnants of dinner still in front of me while my wife, Stacia, washed dishes at the sink. Even after three years together, I still couldn't believe that I was married to this amazing woman with the beautiful butt, although at the moment, I was on the verge of pissing her off by not helping her with the dishes. In an attempt to remedy the situation, I jumped up and handed her a bowl, and in doing so, I brushed against her, the dimensions of our small apartment not giving me a lot of room to move. I can't say that it was entirely accidental, and I lingered there a little longer than was necessary to let her feel how hard my cock was. She humored me for a moment by grinding her ass against my throbbing bulge until I moaned into her hair. Then she reached back with a soapy hand and squeezed me so hard that I almost came in my pants.

I trailed my lips downward and nipped at her neck, leaving a wet mark on her skin. Tracing her jawline with kisses, I moved my hands up to her breasts, which I squeezed until her nipples stiffened. She continued grinding against my cock like she does when we're in bed, so I lowered my hands to the waistband of her pants with the intention of undoing her fly. I figured that we would be leaving the dishes for later and heading directly to the bedroom, but to my surprise, she pushed me away.

"Not so fast," she said, gesturing to the still-messy kitchen. Confused, I thought back to a few nights before when we had let the remnants of a Chinese feast grow cold on our plates while, at my insistence, I took her from behind. I didn't think I could persuade her this time, so, urged on by my dick and a raging libido, I began working double time drying dishes as she handed them to me, putting them away and wiping down the counter and tabletop.

My chores complete, I got back behind my wife, too impatient to take things into the bedroom even though it was only a few feet away. Wrapping my arms around her slender waist, I resumed kissing her neck. I made another attempt at her fly, turning us both around so that we were facing the table. Finally able to get her pants undone, I got on my knees as I lowered them down her hips, taking her panties, too, until they were both at her ankles. As Stacia stepped out of the unwanted garments, kicked them aside and parted her legs, I paused to take in what has to be the most beautiful sight in the world: my wife's dripping wet pussy and perfect ass.

Taking hold of my wife's hips, I breathed in the deliciously heady odor of her musk, and my mouth began to water. I swiped my tongue over her velvety labia, which elicited a moan from Stacia, so I did it again. This time, I took a long lap along her perineum, right up to the pinkish rosebud of her anus. It contracted as I licked a slow circle around it, and then it relaxed as I reached up and teased it lightly with my index finger. Since her opening was slick with my saliva and ready for the invasion, I could slide in easily, but I took my time by only inserting the tip at first and wiggling it around. Then I pushed in to the top knuckle and finally, after pausing for a moment as Stacia's body jerked a bit, I pressed in the rest of the way. As my bottom knuckle touched her cheeks, her asshole closed around my digit and held it tightly, so before I could thrust back in, I had to worm my way back out.

Stacia gasped loudly, announcing her pleasure and conveying her need for more. I was happy to oblige, and my dick sprang up as soon as I removed my jeans. Naked from the waist down, I reclaimed my place behind my wife and rubbed my hardness against her backside. Sighing, she swayed her ass back and forth as I repositioned myself so that my cock was wedged between her buttocks. My dick pulsed impatiently as I looked around the kitchen for a suitable substitute for lube, not wanting to run to the bedroom for the bottle in the nightstand drawer. Finally, I caught sight of the olive oil, so I poured a generous amount into my palm, slowly withdrew from my wife's cheeks, and slicked up.

Next, I splashed some more oil onto my fingers, which I used to massage Stacia's anus. When I brushed against the center, her hole opened slightly as she lurched backward in an attempt to impale herself. I held still, allowing her to fill herself to the bottommost knuckle of one of my digits, and then she paused so I could massage her smooth inner canal. Her body quaked slightly with the pleasure of those intense sensations, but wanting to take things to the next level, I pulled my finger away.

Using both hands, I spread her cheeks wide and positioned my dick at the rosy bud. With the slightest pressure, my mushroom-shaped head popped through the tight ring and was quickly followed by my remaining length. Thanks to my wife's willingness and the copious amount of oil, I was soon all the way in to my balls, which came to rest against her upper thighs. Pressed flat, they throbbed lightly in the moments before I drew out and then thrust back in, burying myself fully again.

Stacia moaned as I plunged repeatedly into her rear hole, so I knew that she was enjoying the way my dick was stretching her. Her sphincter clutched my cock as I gripped her hips more tightly and increased my pace so I was slamming into her butt. Our bodies slapped together as I jackhammered into her ass, and although the table rocked beneath our weight and the force of my thrusting hips, it remained upright.

My wife began shaking just like the table's legs as I kept

pumping into her, though her ass never stopped sucking in my length. Periodically, I'd pull out all the way and then plunge right back in to my aching balls. I knew my orgasm couldn't be far off, but it was my partner's climax that was threatening to arrive soon. She'd snuck a hand down to toggle her clit, and I felt her wobble as she went weak in the knees. I tightened my hold on her hips to keep her upright. Gasping for air, she moaned my name whenever she caught her breath, and then her sphincter spasmed around my shaft.

She cried out as her body went stiff, and then she slumped over on the table as she began quaking with orgasmic tremors. I started fucking her even harder. However, I was only able to slide between her cheeks a few more times before my balls boiled over and sent my cream deep into her derriere.

I ceased moving, my dick buried in my wife as my load flowed into her. As I held her tightly, her body shook and she drew in deep, uneven breaths. My shaft pulsed a few more times, sending more of my seed into her core, milked forth by the contractions of her asshole. Then, as my balls sent forth the last of their contents, her anus relaxed its grip. I was still hard so I remained inside her for a moment longer, but eventually I started getting soft and pulled out. When I took a step back and glanced at my wife's ass, I saw remnants of semen dripping down her thigh.

I reached for a still-damp dish towel to wipe up the sticky streaks, but she pushed my hand away and suggested that we head straight to bed. Since it wasn't even nine o'clock, I knew what that meant: she was ready for a second round. The mischievous look in her eyes confirmed it. My cock, which was still flaccid, gave a little twitch, but I still wasn't sure that I'd be able to get it up again so soon. When

I voiced this concern to my wife, she told me not to worry; my getting hard wouldn't be a problem.

I was intrigued, so I followed her down the hallway, my eyes glued to her swaying backside the entire time. I turned on the light when we reached our bedroom, but she turned it right off. She was obviously taking control; when she told me to take off my shirt and get into bed, I did as she directed. Then she went into the bathroom to freshen up. I heard water running, as well as drawers opening and closing. My thoughts raced as I tried to figure out what she could be up to. Hundreds of possibilities crossed my mind, but none of them came close to what she actually had planned for me.

Although the room was dark, when she finally joined me again, I could tell that she had removed the rest of her clothes and was wearing nothing but a towel wrapped around her torso. Suddenly, all I wanted to do was touch her beautiful tits, so I reached out for her terry-cloth covering and attempted to pull it off. Eluding me, she climbed onto the mattress, knelt at my side, and bent over to press her lips against mine. I thrust my tongue into her mouth, and as we kissed, I ran my fingers over her knee and then started trailing them farther north, her pussy being my ultimate destination. However, I hadn't made it more than an inch beneath the bottom hem of the towel before she pushed my hand off of her leg and told me to roll over onto my side, facing away from her.

Stacia was acting mysteriously, and to be honest, her cagey behavior was making me hot. I felt the warmth in my balls even before my cock started to stir once more, although I hadn't made it much farther than half-mast before she tossed her towel to the floor, lay down behind me, and gave me the surprise of my life. Her body was now flush against mine, and the thing that gave me a jolt wasn't her hand reaching around for my dick but the unfamiliar hardness pressing against my rear.

My revived erection was as hard as the plastic phallus butting against my ass. I wondered how long Stacia had been planning this as she squeezed my stiffening rod and a drop of precome oozed from the tip. Apparently, my body thought that it was going to once again get the opportunity to burrow into her warm, tight ass, but this time, that wasn't on the menu. It was clear that I would be taking it from the other end for the first time in my life. The thought was making me giddy and my cock as hard as stone.

Stacia retained her hold on my shaft as I shifted onto my back to get a good look at her. She was completely naked save for the leather harness that wound around her waist and fastened at one hip. It looked a lot like one of her G-strings except for the four-inch latex dildo that jutted out from its front. When she turned around at my urging, I could see that another strap ran from the black triangle that covered her pussy and bisected her cheeks.

I continued staring in wonder at my naughty wife's midsection as she reached into the nightstand and pulled out the tube of lube. As I watched closely, she smeared a generous amount onto the ersatz cock that bobbed beneath her flat stomach, and then she reached for me. Although I knew better, my body surrendered to instinct and my ass rose up off the sheets in expectation of having my dick pumped by her fist. Instead, she headed south to work a finger between my buttocks. Her target was my anus, which contracted as she trailed over my perineum before stopping at the crinkled bud. Tentatively, she pressed against it, and when it refused to open, she leaned forward once again to give me another kiss. There was no resistance there, and our tongues danced as she continued stroking my hole. Finally, I relaxed, and she slipped her fingertip into me.

The remainder of her finger followed, and I let out a long, deep sigh when she was buried up to her knuckle. She massaged me from inside, gently stroking my pliant canal, and I trembled and let out a whimper. I had never reacted that way to any sort of stimulation, and I wondered if I'd be able to control myself when she actually fucked me with that rubber dick. I didn't have long to think about it because she was already clutching the base of her shaft with her free hand and repositioning herself so that she was kneeling between my thighs, which she'd spread wide open.

Helpless to do anything else, I gazed upward at my wife as she began pressing the plastic cockhead against my asshole. I raised my hips and angled my body, nervous but eager to have her take me. I sucked a breath between my teeth as the shaft—which was about an inch and a half in diameter—gradually filled my rear passage. Then, when the leather harness was flush against my cheeks, I released my breath with a hiss, only to suck it back in when Stacia pulled back out until only the crown remained lodged inside my anus.

Stacia's hands were on my knees, but she paused and slid one into the front of her thong. I couldn't believe that not only was she going to fuck my ass, she would be finger-fucking herself at the same time! "Let me do that," I implored, reaching out to grab her wrist, but she shook her head and gave me a naughty smile. A second later, the sound of muffled buzzing filled the room, revealing to me the special feature of her harness: a secret compartment that housed a small vibrator, leaving our hands free to roam.

Inspired by the vibrator, my wife began fucking me in earnest. Once again, she took hold of my knees to steady herself as she pressed her hips forward to push slowly into my ass and then, just as slowly, moved her hips back to pull the toy right out. She repeated this numerous times, her cock's unrelenting crown never failing to locate my sensitive prostate so that I was panting and moaning in joyful agony. And I wasn't the only one; though she was making considerably less noise than I was, I could tell by her shut-tight eyes and gaping mouth that my wife was having as much fun as I was.

In fact, I was surprised by how much I liked the unceasing invasion; I even pulled my knees up to my chest to give her better access. Seeing that, Stacia picked up her pace, sawing the dildo into my asshole faster and faster until she was fucking me so hard that her breasts bounced with each thrust. I reached out to take hold of those heaving mounds of flesh, and her nipples grazed my palms. Her response was to ram into me even harder and gasp more loudly, and our bodies kept slapping together while the vibrator buzzed away at her clit. I was soon lost in ecstasy, and even though my dick had been neglected for some time by then, no attention was necessary because the pressure of the dildo against my prostate was enough to make me come. But then she took hold of my shaft and began pumping it up and down, sending my arousal even higher.

I didn't know how much more I could take. I began shaking uncontrollably as my wife slammed deep into my asshole, and the vibrations from the toy pressing against her pussy soon did their trick on her. I knew it wouldn't be long before I reached my peak, and in order to make sure she was there with me, I pinched her nipples between my thumbs and forefingers. Stacia reacted immediately; she threw back her head, let out a squeal, and plunged the dildo into me one more time. Her body went stiff for a moment and then she started to quake. Meanwhile, I was seconds away from reaching my own bliss.

The nonstop buzzing of my wife's vibrator kept her cresting again and again, and the other half of that toy soon had me riding the waves of my own pleasure. My balls drew in tightly as I continued to enjoy the feeling of the rubber phallus lodged deep in my butt. The delightful and insistent pressure caused a flood of creamy-white seed to rush up my shaft and through my cockhead to spurt into the air like a geyser. That was followed by a second explosion, and the sticky mess puddled on my stomach and my patch of pubic curls. As Stacia opened her eyes and caught her breath, she ran her fingers through the evidence of my orgasm and regarded me carefully, as though trying to ascertain the effectiveness of her experiment.

In my opinion, it had been a huge success. Though my erection began to flag, hers stayed firm as we disengaged and she turned off the vibrator and unbuckled her leather belt. There was a look of smug satisfaction on her face as she tossed the harness aside and settled in next to me, though whether it was in response to single-handedly engineering two mighty orgasms or from turning the tables for the first time, I couldn't say. The only thing that I was sure of was that it wasn't the last time I'd see that strap-on cock, and just thinking about it made my asshole twitch.

Sassy Seductress

STEPHEN DUNN

When I first met Lynne, I was an inexperienced lover with a pretty conventional approach to sex. My conservative upbringing was partly responsible, as was the fact that my first girlfriend was the same way—content not to push any boundaries. Lynne, however, was a whole new ball game. We were both twenty-four, but she had more experience and more eclectic tastes when it came to sex. In fact, she loved—and still loves—to do the kinds of things that I used to think of as daring and taboo. And most of all, Lynne loves anal sex.

I'll admit that the idea of fucking Lynne in the ass excited me, but I was hesitant when the subject first came up. It didn't help that I am, well, unusually well-endowed. I'm not bragging; I actually wished I wasn't so large when Lynne revealed her passion for anal sex. She's a small girl, bordering on petite, with gorgeous 34B tits, slender hips, a flat stomach, and a tight, tiny ass; I didn't see how she could accommodate my cock back there. She tried to assure me that my large size only made her more eager to try. There was a playful but determined glint in her eyes as she said, "Before the month is out, you and I will have such an incredibly good time with your cock in my ass that you'll wonder how you ever did without."

When she said that, my prick leaped in my pants. I realized that I might not need much convincing, after all. But Lynne had an action plan that she wanted to carry out, and I was more than happy to see where it led us.

I didn't have long to wait. The very next night, as we were finishing dinner at her place, Lynne ran a hand through her blonde, shoulder-length hair and explained that she had enrolled us in a sex seminar the following Saturday. "The description on the website says anal sex techniques will be one of the topics," she explained with a coquettish grin. Amused, curious, and excited all at once, I agreed to go. In the meantime, Stage One of her plan would begin immediately. Lynne headed down the hall toward her bedroom saying, "I want to show you something." I followed her, enjoying the movement of her sexy ass.

Lynne started up an album on her bedside stereo dock. Her bawdy striptease, perfectly matched to the music's driving beat, made my dick as hard as stone in no time. When she was completely naked, Lynne reached under her bed and pulled out a beat-up old box. We had only been dating for a couple of months, so I didn't yet know about her impressive collection of sex toys. She had all kinds of vibrators, dildos, butt plugs, and anal beads. Taking one of the smaller dildos and a bottle of lube from the box, she lay back against the headboard, greased up the toy, and spread her legs, presenting her completely shaved cunt and asshole to my hungry eyes. Then she pressed the dildo to her back door and eased it in, watching my reaction. With her free hand, she began to rub her pussy as she slid the toy inside her ass.

Lynne proceeded to demonstrate her skill with a variety of anal intruders, replacing each one with a bigger one after a few minutes to gradually expand her sphincter. Soon she was moaning and squirming with deep-rooted pleasure. Watching her, I felt my pulse quicken; I opened my pants and stroked myself. When she reached for a long, thick vibrator that was about as big as my dick, I thought she must be kidding. I stared as the lifelike head vanished into her hole. She paused a moment, treasuring the sensation, then packed the rest of the thing inch by inch into her ass, until only the flared base was visible. It was a breathtaking sight. Her fingers strummed her clit faster and faster, as if she were playing the climax of a guitar riff. The big vibrator moved in and out of her ass four times before she came with a long, hoarse cry, hips bouncing and ass muscles clenching.

As Lynne's climax began to subside, she giggled sexily and welcomed me atop her while continuing to work the vibrator in and out of her rear hole. We had great sex that night, but by unspoken agreement, we delayed the anal deed for just a little longer, so Lynne could carry out Stage Two—the sex seminar. Anticipation is sweet indeed.

Saturday finally came, and I drove to Lynne's place to pick her up. She answered the door in a clinging T-shirt and a skirt that showed off her fine legs. She seemed a little cagey during the drive, as if she had a secret. I chalked it up to nervousness about the class, since neither of us really knew what to expect.

The instructor was a smart, attractive woman in her forties who put us at ease with her relaxed manner and engaging wit. Over the next three hours, she explained to the fifteen or so couples in the class how we could expand our sexual lives and explore new techniques for pleasure. When she turned to anal sex, everyone seemed to lean forward in their seats. The instructor talked about the importance of lube, communication between partners, and ideal positions for backdoor sex, using a slide show to illustrate her descriptions. Several people had questions or shared their own advice. It was a real eye-opener, not to mention a turn-on, to see that so many people were interested in trying anal sex or improving the ass play they were already having.

I had a huge erection by the time the class ended. I couldn't wait to get back to Lynne's place and give her what she desperately wanted. In the car, she guided my free hand up her skirt so I could feel how wet her panties were.

We had barely stepped through her front door when Lynne pulled me to the living room couch and started tugging at my clothes. I took over the job and quickly got myself naked, but not as fast as Lynne, who made even shorter work of her shirt, shoes, skirt, and underwear. "What about Stage Three?" I rasped.

"This is it," she said huskily. We knelt on the couch together, and her small hand clasped the thick shaft of my manhood. She bent to lap up the drop of precome glistening on my cock's bulbous tip. I reached for her sun-kissed tits, tan lines revealing Lynne's taste in ultra-skimpy swimwear. Her erect nipples were vivid nubs of pink atop each breast's creamy zenith.

Lynne sat with her legs tucked beneath her and spent a couple of minutes demonstrating her ardent affection for my cock. Her hands and tongue slid up and down the taut skin, making my shaft shiny and wet. Then she stretched her lips over my thick glans and bobbed, her head rising and falling, making me shudder. Finally she sat back, smiling broadly, and turned to show me her naked ass. That's when I remembered the mysterious air she'd had on the way to the seminar, because now her secret was revealed: the circular base of a butt plug emerged from between her asscheeks. She had put it in before leaving home, anticipating the inevitable. Lynne looked back at me over her shoulder and laughed with delight.

"You've been wearing it all day?" I asked.

She nodded. "I wanted to be ready for you." With that, she hurried into the bedroom and came back with her trusty bottle of lube. Once again she offered me her backside, and I carefully withdrew the plug. It was smooth, pliant silicone, and surprisingly thick. Just thinking of Lynne walking around and sitting in that class all afternoon with the toy in her ass made my cock grow an extra half inch. Lynne was on the couch, ass high in the air, waiting for me. I dove into her spread cleft and lustily snacked on both her holes. She moaned and squirmed as I slid my tongue back and forth between her sopping cunt and her puckered anus.

Eventually, I settled in at her asshole and traced wet circles around the wrinkly skin, prompting an even louder moan from my girlfriend. With my hands flat against her buttcheeks, I dipped my tongue inside that forbidden orifice. "Yes," Lynne cried, "that's so good!" Her fingertips were playing at her cunt, ramping up the sensations, and soon she grew impatient for my cock. Turning to lie on her back, she said, "I've got to have your dick in me. You know where to put it, Steve. It's time to fuck my ass." Her eyes were bright with feverish desire.

I was ready—god, was I ever! Pausing first to spread an ample amount of lube on my dick, I pulled Lynne's hips up against me and prepared to penetrate her tiny sphincter. An inch higher, her pussy was glossy with the wetness of her desire. My pulse raced at the sight. The bulging head of my tool still looked frighteningly large as it knocked at the door of her ass. Using both hands, Lynne spread herself wide. I took a deep breath and gently pushed forward.

Amazingly, Lynne's anal opening accepted my bulky knob with relative ease and sealed up just behind the crown. I'd never felt anything as velvety tight and warm before; it was pure heaven. "Ooh," Lynne said, adjusting to the sensation. Then she sighed with sublime pleasure. "That's a big cock. Go ahead now, nice and slow."

I eased deeper inside her, my gaze riveted on the intersection of my penis and her wide-stretched anus. Lynne grunted and closed her eyes. I felt her ring of muscle relax slightly and pushed onward, feeding more of myself into her hungry asshole. A sheen of sweat appeared on Lynne's face and chest. "Oh—oh—oh," she stammered. "Stuff that beautiful cock into me!"

I took another minute to squeeze the rest of my length into her, until I had nothing more to give. I stared, feeling almost giddy at the sight of my pelvis flush against Lynne's tight ass. A peal of wonder and delight erupted from her throat. Holding on to Lynne's legs, I eased out, all the way to the head, and then sawed back in to the hilt. "Yes, yes!" she practically screamed, encouraging me to move faster, then faster still, plundering her luscious butt. I hadn't thought it possible, but there I was, pumping my wood in and out of her ass, and both of us loving every second of it. Lynne's tits trembled with the shock of each thrust. I bent low between her upraised legs and sucked her erect nipples, feeling the rapid beat of her heart with my lips.

Before long, I felt that telltale kick in my groin, and I knew the exquisite end was coming. How I'd even lasted that long was a mystery to me. At about the same time, I saw Lynne's face contort with a rush of unbelievable pleasure as she fingered her swollen clit. This time, though, her orgasm was something different than anything I'd seen before, something off the charts. She went nearly still for a long moment, eyes wide with surprise, and a high-pitched keen of joy issued from her throat. Then she succumbed to a wave of deep tremors that rumbled through her small frame and kept on rumbling, building in intensity. Her honey streamed down from her cunt, coating my dick, and I felt her anus flex and squeeze, gripping me and milking the semen from my balls until finally great spurts of come erupted from my dick deep inside her ass. I grunted and groaned like a madman for half a minute, jerking into Lynne's rear end until we were both completely spent.

We shared a sweaty embrace. "I can't wait to try that again," she whispered at last. I laughed and rolled off her, not realizing just how soon she meant. Lynne headed for the bathroom, and a moment later I heard the bathwater running. I grabbed a bottle of champagne from the refrigerator and joined her in the tub, where we passed the bottle back and forth, toasting our first anal encounter. Later, we watched a movie while dining on chow mein, sesame chicken, and egg rolls. All the while, however, our incredible afternoon tryst was never far from our minds.

It was late when Lynne stood up from the couch and announced she was going to bed. I took a few minutes to tidy up the kitchen, and then followed her into the bedroom. She was lying on her stomach on the bed, her beautiful nude body practically glowing with arousal in the light of the bedside lamp. The full-length mirrors on the closet doors presented another view of her sublime form. She had one hand hidden beneath her hips and was beckoning me with the other, offering a smile that was both affectionate and lewd.

My cock rapidly swelled to life. "You're insatiable," I said, shedding my T-shirt and boxers.

Lynne withdrew her hand from her crotch and held up fingers shiny with her juices. "Look how wet I am for you."

I covered the distance between us in two quick strides and sprawled on the bed beside her. She climbed atop me, planting her knees on either side of my head so her plush pussy lips were directly over my face. I paused to admire her glistening pink folds for a moment before reaching out to tease them with my tongue. Her inner labia opened like a flower to me, dripping hotly onto my lips. Lynne, meanwhile, had flattened her body to mine and was zestily sucking my cock. Lifting my head a bit, I looked between her thighs and saw her breasts crushed against my stomach. I felt her lips slide along the underside of my cock and down to my balls, which she gathered into her mouth like a pair of big marbles. For a minute, she licked and sucked my sac with divine skill, and then I felt her moving lower still. I couldn't believe how good her tongue felt as she probed and prodded my private hole. Delicious tingles spread through my ass and groin. I returned the favor, licking between Lynne's spread buttocks and moistening her nether opening.

After a minute, Lynne sat up and moved to squat over my shaft. I caressed her hips and her back as she sank down, slowly filling her pussy. Languidly at first, and then more fervently, she raised and lowered herself on me, taking lusty pleasure in the effort to fit as much of my mammoth pole inside herself as possible. Her thighs and hips flexed sumptuously as she lifted and lowered, her cunt sucking me like a hungry, wet mouth.

But this was not the endgame that Lynne had in mind. My own excitement intensified sharply a moment later when she raised up off my drenched cock and replanted it between her asscheeks. Holding those supple globes apart, she impaled herself once more, this time taking my rod into her tiniest hole. With each inch that disappeared inside, Lynne let out a grunt of acute satisfaction. We were both facing the mirror, and when I peered around her tanned thigh, I could see her watching our reflection, transfixed by the white-hot view of my fat cock as it stretched her orifice. I had never seen such a look of wonder and passion on her face. She shuddered as she reached the base of my dick. Leaning back over my chest, she began to ride me. I reached around her jerking hips and rubbed my palm over her swollen labia. She was so slick there, she was almost gooey, like a melting marshmallow. I found her clit and ran my fingers across it gently at first, then more roughly, as Lynne demanded. She was bouncing on me with unremitting energy, slapping her butt down on my groin to drive my penis in deep. All that violent friction brought me quickly to the cusp. I grabbed Lynne around the waist and came mightily, feeling the semen pulse out of my cock. Before I was through, I realized that she was coming, too. A string of incoherent curses accompanied her undulations, which rose and fell in strength but never quite stopped entirely.

"More," Lynne was saying as she ground against me. She couldn't get enough. She rolled onto her side and I rolled with her, our bodies spooning. For the moment, I was still rock hard inside her.

"Fuck—my—ass," she urged, emphasizing each word with a sharp push of her butt back at me. I did as she said, squeezing her asscheeks and rocking into her, splitting her rear end with my dick. Lynne's anus was nicely relaxed by now, and I pumped briskly into that responsive opening. I held her upper leg high so we could see the action reflected in the mirror, and she became even more excited, if that was at all possible. Whatever words she uttered next were incoherent as she bucked against me. She reached back, stroking her ass, then slid her hand to our flash point and spread her fingers around my thrusting cock as she ground her clit against her palm. Her cries grew louder and deeper until finally, sobbing triumphantly, she came completely unglued. I drilled into her palpitating hole a minute longer, bedsprings protesting loudly as the orgasmic tempest buffeted my lover's body. Then something truly remarkable happened: I felt myself coming for the third time in a day, which had never happened to me before. The unstoppable flow surged rapidly and overwhelmed me. I roared out Lynne's name and slammed tightly against her, firing the last traces of my cream into the depths of her ass. That silky hole drew all it could from me, sucking up every last drop.

Lynne finally rolled onto her stomach with a contented smile. "My anal debutant is now a pro," she whispered. As I collapsed next to her, my well-worked cock slipped free of her ass, and a little bit of my come oozed out, too. I gave Lynne a hug and closed my eyes, feeling transformed. My sexy girlfriend had opened the door to an exciting new world for both of us to enjoy, and I planned to explore every bit of it with her.

Atlantic Tides

Piper Williams

The green suburbs of Long Island rolled past the windows, gradually giving way to smaller towns and resort communities as the train headed east. I remembered my girlhood trips out here years ago with my family, when farms bordered the tracks and the famous Long Island ducklings outnumbered the people. Although it was much more built up now, there were still places that seemed never to change. Jeff's house at Quogue was one of them—a gingerbread Victorian cottage that had been added to over the years in various styles or lack of them. He had brought me there for the first time six years ago, and I had fallen in love with its ramshackle charm.

I'd fallen in love with Jeff a few months earlier, when we met at the opera. A heated debate on the merits of the stand-in soprano had led first to coffee and brandy, then to a series of dates and a torrid love affair. We were somewhat calmer these days, used to being an established couple, but when we were apart for any length of time I missed him desperately. A shiver went through me at the thought of his big hands clutching my ass and pulling me to him, and the vibration of the train had me buzzing with arousal.

Jeff was the first man who had taught me the erogenous potential of my ass, and I was aching to feel his thick cock inside me there. He'd been in Europe on business for three weeks, and I was wild with desire. The train clanked into the little stop, and I hopped off carrying only my briefcase. Everything else I needed for my visit was already at the house.

There he was, leaning against his battered old "Hamptons Heap." He looked like the handsomest beachcomber the Atlantic tides had ever washed ashore. His honey-blond hair fell over his eyes, as usual a little too long, and he'd gotten a good start on growing a beard. It was darker than his hair and accented his strong jaw in a way I found irresistible.

He stood there for a second, looking me up and down, and then opened his arms and hugged me. His mouth locked on to mine, and we seemed to be vying to draw breath from each other for a long moment before we stepped back to say hello. We got into the car and drove the mile or so to his house. The scruffy black-and-white, semidomesticated cat that owned all the humans in the neighborhood trotted across the driveway, tail aloft in salute as we pulled in. Domesticity was restored. I was where I belonged.

I went upstairs to shower and change while Jeff grilled a couple of steaks and threw together a salad. Over glasses of wine we caught up on news before we cleared away the dishes and headed up to bed. The sun had hardly set, but we were too hungry for each other to wait any longer.

I slid off his shirt and unzipped his jeans, pulling them down over his lean hips to reveal his already half-hard cock. Sinking to my knees, I took its base in one hand and his balls in the other. My lips kissed the dark head before I ran my tongue around its flange and took it into my mouth. His sweet-salt taste was familiar and very dear—for all that, I seemed never to be able to remember it exactly right. At the first caress of my tongue a quiver ran through his muscled thighs, and I swallowed him to the root, caressing his balls.

His shaft grew and thickened in my mouth, stretching into my throat, and soon Jeff was fully hard. His hands tangled through my hair, and he gently pushed me off his erection. He guided me over to the bed, disposing of my shift in one graceful movement. I was naked beneath it.

We fell into the big old bed and twined ourselves together, hands and mouths reestablishing ownership of favorite curves and hollows, until Jeff slid down my body and kissed the moist thatch between my thighs. I gasped at the warmth of his breath and moaned as his tongue found its way between my labia, seeking the ripening bud of my clit. My whole being was transfixed with the electric pleasure of it, and I lifted my hips to meet him.

One hand slipped under my ass and his strong fingers parted my cheeks, seeking the other bud that was eager to open to his caress. His tongue darted downward, slickening my back hole with its teasing flicks. A fingertip teased my anus, making me groan with longing before Jeff took pity and worked it inside. I clenched around the welcomed invader, wanting to close him in as tightly as possible. Jeff's tongue continued its irresistible motions on my clit, taking my pleasure higher. My first orgasm caught me unawares, and the rhythmic shocks ran down around his finger, clutching and releasing it.

Honey seeped from my slit to ease his finger's passage, and he now worked a second digit into my opening. I was dying to have his cock inside me, and I begged for it almost incoherently. Jeff's fingers left my ass, and he moved up to kneel between my legs. Reaching over to the side table, he pumped out a dollop of lube and applied it first to his cock, then to my asshole.

Jeff lifted my ass, encouraging me to rest my legs on his shoulders, and for a moment he was poised with his magnificent cock only grazing my longing rosebud. Then, with a sureness born of long acquaintance, he pushed forward, burying his cockhead and shoving his thick meat deep inside me. For that inevitable split second, I was sure that I was insane—there was no way he could fit that enormous tool into the tight confines of my anus. Then he was inside me, past the instinctive closing off of muscles, filling me heart-deep.

I almost began to cry; he felt so good. The smooth strength of my muscles held him close, and then he began to fuck me, picking up speed and force as he saw I wanted more.

My hands clutched at him and slapped at his ass to drive him deeper, harder. Our flesh fought, and his was winning the mastery over me. My insides gave themselves over to his relentless rhythm, and then I was aware of my body softening and warming on his driving shaft, like a kid glove melting around him.

I cried out as I came, barely conscious that his thumb had, all this while, been stroking my clit. I was drowning in a wave of red and gold, falling into a starburst of sensation that centered in my throbbing sex. His cock seemed to swell and my flesh stretched with it, clinging to him as he reared up and plunged one last time, spilling his come into my depths.

We stayed like that for an unending moment, and then collapsed, my legs swinging down to one side and his cock sliding out of me as he curled his body around the softness of my asscheeks. Jeff's ragged breathing stirred the tendrils of hair on the back of my neck, and his strong arms held me close. I quickly sank into the oblivion of sleep.

Morning found us sprawled together, still sticky and disheveled. We laughed at the odd spikes my hair had gotten pushed into by our fucking, and I swatted Jeff with my pillow when he tried to tickle me. He reached for me again, but I eluded him and ran into the bathroom, diving into the shower before he could get a good hold.

Jeff soon followed me into the steaming water, and we washed each other thoroughly, teasing happy moans from each other with familiar caresses. As the water cascaded over us, I went down on my knees and took him in my mouth, backing him up against the wall of the shower and refusing to let go. It didn't take much persuasion for his cock to get as hard as ever, hitting the back of my throat as I bobbed up and down on it. I ran my tongue up the sensitive underside of his shaft and squeezed his balls as I plunged forward again. He stiffened and shot his load into my throat, and I swallowed it hungrily.

We finished our shower more sedately and threw on T-shirts and shorts before hopping into the car for a picnic breakfast on the beach. We got coffee and croissants on the way, with a jar of our favorite thick raspberry jam, and devoured the lot lying on the white sand, watching the sea beat against the shore.

Jeff rolled over to me and pinned me against the blanket, scattering crumbs all around us. I was glad I'd had the presence of mind to put the lid back on the jam. No one was around, and Jeff unzipped my shorts, pushing his hand between my legs and holding me still with his other arm. His mouth sealed mine, and his fingers opened my pussy, stroking down on my clit as he finger-fucked me deeper and deeper. I tried to buck to meet him, but he held me fast, forcing me to surrender to his ruthless pursuit of my climax. Finally, it burst over me, and I writhed until the shocks subsided.

"Take me home," I whispered heatedly in his ear. "I want to have you without a lot of sand between us."

Minutes later we were back in his sunny bedroom, stripped and laughing as I pushed him down on the bed and straddled his torso. He pulled my pussy down onto his face as I sank my mouth around his cock, and we devoured each other as hungrily as we had our alfresco breakfast. He had me on fire with the need to come again, but I was at that point where my clit was almost too sensitive to be touched. Pulling away, I turned and faced him, holding his erection in my hands.

"Just lie there," I commanded. "I want to play." Jeff knew me in this mood, and he folded his hands behind his head, ready for me to pleasure us both.

I straddled his hips and ran the head of his cock up and down the moist cleft between my labia, fucking its little slit with my engorged clitoris, teasing us both unmercifully. Before we'd had quite enough, I lowered myself onto his shaft, the soft walls of my vagina enclosing his velvet-covered steel rod. Rocking myself back and forth as I rode him, I could feel my cunt getting wetter and slicker and my whole body tensing before the dam broke and my orgasm washed over me.

Still quivering from the sweet violence of my climax, I rose and thrust my hips forward, pulling my ass over his cock. In one motion I sank down on it, impaling my ass on his slickened shaft and fucking myself with his flesh. I was about to burst with the need to be ravished, to be invaded, and I wore out my knees riding his cock, unable to drive him into me with the force I craved.

Jeff grabbed my hips to slow me down, then lifted me off him and flipped me over, my hips raised over a pillow. His hand came down on my cheek with a crack, leaving a fiery handprint. Prying my cheeks apart, he slicked up my rear hole with lube, and then his cock was driving into my ass again—but this time his weight was holding me helpless beneath him and I was indeed being ravished by his thick shaft. I could no longer tell where I ended and he began, though I was all softness and he was all implacable steel.

I fought to raise my hips to meet him, and his hands pulled at my hips, yanking me against his groin, scraping his wiry pubic hair against my ass and his balls slapping against my cunt. I was out of my mind with the pure delight of surrender.

With one hand he held mine captive above my head, and his teeth bit gently into my shoulder. He moved a little, just to remind me of his possession of my ass, then pulled me up on my hands and knees without losing his place inside me.

My ass convulsed around him, and I buried my face in the pillow, my hands clutching at the sheet. Again his hand cracked across my rounded bottom and his fingers dug into my hips as he slammed forward, driving even deeper with a nearly crazed indifference to anything around him but the wildly responsive flesh of my ass. His fingers reached for my nipple and twisted it, the blissful pain driving me over the edge. I gave up counting, gave up even thinking of this as orgasm. I was one great bonfire of desire and fulfillment. I rammed my ass back at him, writhing in total abandon.

I felt him stiffen, his muscles quivering, and then he rammed me even harder, knocking me flat into the pillows as he poured his load into me. I experienced every spasm as though it were my own, and when he was still, I clenched my sated muscles around his receding cock, reluctant to let him go. Muzzily, I was aware of his slipping out of me and whispering, "I love you," in my ear.

How long I lay there, pliant as melting butter, I'm not entirely sure. My next conscious sensation was the smell of strong coffee wafting toward my nose. I stretched sleepily, feeling the consequences of his debauched depredations in every nerve ending. Rolling over, I smiled up at him. Clasping my arms around his neck and pulling his face down to mine, I whispered mischievously, "I think you must have missed me almost as much as I missed you."

Hide and Go Anal

JOHN ROBERTS

Fuck a woman in the ass? Why? Up until recently, I considered myself that rare male who could honestly say he'd never thought seriously about anal sex. It wasn't ever a possibility with the women I'd gone out with, and to me the idea just seemed…unnecessary. Why an asshole when a perfectly useful and desirable pussy was right there?

Then I met Brandi.

We had a mutual friend, Tim, a loud, moneyed guy who likes to host lavish parties. He has a place in the country, and I found myself free for the weekend when I received one of his coveted invitations.

"Come on, Johnny!" he bellowed cheerfully over the phone. "It'll do you good to get away from the goddamn office. Good food, good liquor, good women. I promise—you'll love it!"

When Tim says, "You'll love it," you *want* to love it. His enthusiasm is unstoppable.

I drove out on Saturday, deep into the rural environs. I stepped out of my car and paused to inhale the scents of pine and wildflowers. After the city, the quiet was soothing. It *did* feel good to get away.

Tim's home consists of a main house, a big pool and patio, and outlying bungalows, the whole complex surrounded by untouched forested land. Guests were already on hand when I walked in. Tim bear-hugged me and threw me into the mix. He was grinning like a Roman emperor, directing people toward a buffet and bar. I snagged a cocktail and heard a splash from the pool. I turned around.

A stunning woman in a red bikini was backstroking the length of the pool. Her arms moved in a perfect clockwork, and her long toned legs kicked gracefully. I watched her every move, completely mesmerized. Her bared midriff was tight, with a dime-sized navel, and her firm breasts pushed against red fabric toward the cloudless afternoon sky. Was I being rude? I couldn't stop myself from staring. Her skin had a coppery hue, with subtle golden undertones, and her long dark hair streamed over her shoulders as she cut an unerring course toward the end of the pool where I stood.

I thought she was beautiful even before she slowly and sensually emerged from the water, limbs dripping, hair sleek and straight. I let myself think for the first time that this weekend might be more than a simple getaway.

Before I could introduce myself, she fixed me with frank, dark eyes and said, "Hi there."

"Hi. You were in last summer's Olympics, right? Silvered for the two-hundred meter freestyle, I believe."

"I took the bronze," she replied, running with my joke. "The Russian judge was an asshole." She smiled one of those smiles that make a woman look totally alive and aware.

"My name's John."

"I'm Brandi."

We stayed close as the afternoon became evening, and she momentarily excused herself to change into a loose white top and denim skirt. We talked and grew comfortable with each other. I learned that Brandi ran a nonprofit that interacted often with Tim's businesses. I told her about the legal work I'd done for Tim. But the shoptalk was only a cover. I tried some flirtatious banter, comments that could be tossed aside if they didn't land. As she responded with increasing warmth, I grew a bit bolder. She gave me that smile again, and a prickling of desire ran over my flesh.

A few dozen people were still present as night settled in. The food had been terrific, but by now even the vague formalities of eating were done. The get-together took on a Saturnalian vibe. The booze flowed liberally. Most of the guests had drifted onto the broad patio. The stars shone. The pool lights threw watery shadows everywhere.

I noticed two women lying side by side on a chaise longue. They faced each other, engaged in a long slow kiss. A man came up the steps at the pool's shallow end, naked and grinning, his half-erect cock swinging.

I'd been to Tim's parties before. They usually went this way after a while. Brandi stood at my elbow. I looked at her sidelong, a little leery of her reaction. Her lovely dark eyes were wide but full of a knowing mirth.

"Does this sort of thing bother you?" I asked.

"What—people enjoying themselves?"

"I mean, a bunch of adults behaving like skinny-dipping fools."

"No. Does it trouble *you*, my suddenly prudish man?" Her hand curled around my arm, and she pulled closer to me. I very much liked the feel of her body against mine.

Tim's roaring laugh came from somewhere inside the main house.

"Our host likes fun," I said. "He likes happy guests." It was true. Tim is always generous with his wealth and with the pleasures he can provide others.

"Are you…staying over?" Suddenly, Brandi's face hovered quite near mine.

"I didn't tell Tim one way or the other when I arrived. I didn't arrange to stay overnight in one of the bungalows." I nodded beyond the patio's splashing shadows, to the small structures nestled at the edge of the woods.

Brandi's fingers tightened on my arm. "I did," she said, close enough to me that I felt the brush of her breath on my cheek.

We kissed. It was a simple, lovely contact, and the act finalized what had been steadily building between us. The softness of her lips and firmness of her body enticed me.

More naked people were diving into the pool when we strolled together toward the quaint little outbuilding Tim had earlier assigned to Brandi. I had stayed over at Tim's country place before and knew the layout. We went inside the bungalow, and Brandi fired up a single kerosene-burning lamp. It was a cozy enclosure, with bare beams crisscrossing a low ceiling. A sliding glass door gave onto a small back porch, beyond which stood the ghostly shapes of crowding trees. The furnishings were faux-rustic and very comfortable.

Brandi took my hand and led me toward the iron-framed, quilt-covered bed.

We sat on the edge. My heart quickened, but it was the delicious nervousness of discovery. I liked that we'd had time to chat. I felt I knew this woman, at least enough to recognize her as compassionate and intelligent, as well as extremely attractive.

When we kissed again, it was deeper, a probing of tongues. I put my arms around her. She ground her lips against mine, one hand grazing my cheek, and then sliding around to my nape, grasping, her whole arm pulling me with surprising force. She drew me down on top of her, breaking our kiss. Her fast breaths made her breasts rise and fall beneath the loose top. Her teeth caught my lower lip playfully. I ran my fingers into her still slightly damp hair.

"I want you out of your fucking clothes!" she panted.

I was only taken aback for a second. Then she was helpfully tearing off my shirt and slacks. A physically active lifestyle has kept my body trim and toned. When my hard cock sprang into view, she growled with pleasure. She flung away her top, and I beheld her firm, remarkable tits. A zipper gave a fast, tiny shriek, and her denim skirt went flying. She wore no panties. Her pussy glistened expectantly beneath a cropped dark triangle.

She spread her taut thighs. When I knelt between them, she seized my cock in her strong fist. The flickering lamplight brought out the richest golden hues from her bare skin. Her body was a drum-tight glory of well-used muscles and pleasing feminine curves.

"Fuck me good, John," she begged. "Fuck me like I need it!"

Her words were an exciting cross between candor and sexual aggression. I felt a feral grin stretching my face as she guided my cock to her waiting hole.

I braced my hands on the pillows on either side of her head and thrust deep inside.

The clutching slippery heat shot pleasure all through me. My blood raced in my veins. I drove into her depths, drew out, plunged in again. Her athletic thighs clamped my flanks. She reached a hand around to sink her fingers into the flesh of my ass. She obviously didn't want any slow, subtle buildup, so I pounded her. Fleshy smacks filled the snug room. The iron bed frame squealed. Brandi lifted her hips to meet my every downward lunge. The grip of her pussy was hot and fluid. I felt her trembling all over. She grabbed my ass with her other hand. Her face twisted with the intense exertion of extreme pleasure. I felt sweat dripping off me. Bliss simmered in my balls as they continued to slap her asscheeks.

About halfway toward my own climax, Brandi went into a joyful fit. She thrashed about on the quilt, breasts heaving, a wild cry tearing from her throat.

I rode her through an evidently drastic climax, slowing my thrusts and finally easing to a stop. I gazed down on her, feeling the satisfaction of any sensible man who has brought a woman to orgasm. Now I was assured she had gotten at least a share of the ecstasy that was her due. My own release wasn't too far off.

I'd just started to move my fiercely hard cock inside her again when she abruptly wrenched herself away. I sat back and watched her roll over onto her knees, facing the wall. She stuck two fingers in her mouth, looked at me over her shoulder, and smeared the wet fingertips over the smooth pucker of her asshole. Her dark eyes were alight with a passionate fire.

"Put that big, fat cock in my ass!" she commanded. She gripped the headboard rail and stuck her gorgeously molded backside out toward me.

I blinked at her, feeling lost. "What?"

A flicker of our earlier banter-fueled amusement came to her features. "You don't know what I mean?"

I leaned back a little farther. "I've just never done that."

Brandi heard the honesty in my tone. Sympathy flashed across her face. She let go of the railing and turned. "It feels good, John. I don't apologize for loving anal sex. I like to take a man into me where I feel most vulnerable, where it's like he's touching me in my most secret place. It's a secret I like to share. I'd like to share it with you."

I sat there on my haunches, clueless as to how to explain that I had never wanted to do a woman that way. This magnificent night felt like it was about to slip away from me.

Brandi sensed my hesitation, but seemed to have thought of a solution. "If it's strange for you," she said brightly, "maybe you need some unfamiliar circumstances. You know, to take your mind off whatever's got you so worked up." She was plainly delighted with her idea. She bounced past me, vaulting off the bed to land by the sliding door. "I'll go hide, and you come find me!"

With that, she flung the door open and hurled herself out into the night, leaping from the porch like a gazelle and disappearing immediately into the trees.

I stared. I gaped. I couldn't believe what was happening. But I was still as hard as rock, and I wanted her desperately. After a moment's hesitation, I went out into the night after her.

The day had been warm, but a stark country coolness had replaced it. I stepped off the porch, wincing as my bare soles touched the ground. The air chilled the sweat on my body. I took a few doubtful steps toward the trees.

What the hell was I doing? I was twenty-eight years old, a successful lawyer, and here I was playing hide-and-go-seek with a woman who wanted my dick up her ass. It was crazy.

Funny thing, though, the thought of doing that to her didn't seem quite so shocking anymore. Maybe something in her rhapsodic soliloquy about the joys of anal sex had convinced me the act was worth trying. God knew I still wanted to fuck her, one way or the other.

I could feel that feral grin on my face again as I slipped in among the dark pine trees. I felt terribly exposed. Looking behind, I saw lights inside a couple of the other small bungalows, but already the woods were swallowing me. Starlight dripped silvery shadows onto my bare skin. Where had Brandi gone? How tough was she going to make this game, which I was now determined to win?

After bumping my knee and picking up a minor scratch or two, I stood still and listened. A breeze rustled the leaves. I heard a bird. But I also detected, off to my left, a tiny squeal of girlish laughter.

I moved carefully in that direction. I thought I heard some-one's fast, excited breaths just ahead. Pressing quietly against a tree, I reached around either side of the trunk and seized two bare shoulders. Brandi yelped delightedly.

I stepped around the tree and found her in a clear shaft of moonlight. Her nude form was exquisite. In this setting, she looked like some mystical forest creature. Her dark cascading hair hid her face until she tilted her head up at me.

"I guess I'm *it*," she said, voice husky with need.

I turned her around to face the tree. "Not yet you aren't," I said. Our hide-and-seek wasn't over. This time I dabbed my fingers with spit and slicked up her waiting nether hole again. She shivered at my touch. She reached up and grabbed a branch in each hand, her sculpted ass thrust out toward me.

First, I swirled my cockhead around her ring. I knew that once I was inside her this way, I would be committing a sex act that was brand-new to me. A final flutter of nervousness went through me, but I told myself I was being an idiot.

I slipped my cockhead inside. Her pucker relaxed, seeming to suck me in. I fed her my inches, a little warily. She moaned, and the deeper I went, the louder she got. When my balls were finally flush against the tight curves of her ass, she cried out into the night, "I like you there, John!"

The angle was a little strange. Her channel had a forceful grip on me. I could feel the flex of unfamiliar interior muscles. But this no longer seemed a bizarre act to me.

I closed my hands around her hips and started stroking into her.

The heat inside her was intense. Her passage wasn't as silky as her cunt. Yet it had a sort of rugged smoothness to it. I plunged in again and again, going slowly. There still seemed something fragile about the whole undertaking, and I moved cautiously.

But Brandi put that to rest by looking back at me, eyes blazing. "Fuck me harder! Fuck my ass like you *mean* it!"

I grinned, my fingers tightening over her hip bones. I gave her a merciless thrust, slamming her. She groaned with unmistakable rapture. Dark hair churned back and forth across her golden back as she whipped her head from side to side.

The cool air caressed our bodies, but sweat was streaming anew on me. I saw the sheen of Brandi's flesh in the light shining through the branches. I was aware of how exposed we were, but that only added to the mounting excitement I was experiencing.

She wanted it hard, so I gave it to her that way. I planted my heels in the bare earth, toes gripping fallen leaves, and I hammered into her luscious little asshole. I drove to her ultimate depths each time. The taut halves of her ass rippled with the impact of my thrusts.

As I went at it, I realized that I now understood in some distant corner of my overheated mind what she had been talking about earlier. It felt like I was reaching her in a special place. I was penetrating to the essence of her. Here she was most vulnerable, and here she had invited me. She trusted me to bring her the specific pleasure she so craved.

I was connected to this beautiful woman, cock to ass, and the act was lovely and true and meaningful.

It was also some fan-fucking-tastic sex! I speared Brandi's ass as she hung on to that tree for dear life. My cock blazed in and out of her, gripped by that sweet clenching ring. She was bucking back against me, taking me as deep as humanly possible, wanting as much of me as she could get. I accommodated her. I impaled her with every thrust.

Ecstasy was building in me. I meant to blast this woman's defenseless interior with my hot, salty juice. As I hurtled recklessly toward that release, I felt my body awakening, crackling with carnal electricity. The length of my lunging cock was alive with delight. I had crossed over into a dark exotic land, and now it was time to leave my mark there.

My eyes rolled halfway up into my skull. A wordless cry came from my throat. I heard Brandi's answering yowl scattering through the pine trees. A bird screeched nearby, and for all I know wolves fled the vicinity.

The deep joy took me and lifted me. When my first liquid jet hit, Brandi writhed like crazy, torquing still more delight from me. I spiked her hard with my cock, delivering my seed to her innermost reaches. I did as she'd told me: I fucked her ass like I meant it. Because I *did* mean it. The come I was pumping into her was the proof of my sincerity.

Each spurt rocked me. Heat rolled off the two of us in waves. I stayed joined to her vulnerable, but evidently very durable, passage as the last spasms of euphoria shook me. Eventually, my eyes rolled back down. I staggered back, disengaging, and watched my pearly fluid dribbling down the insides of Brandi's thighs. She still hung on to the branches, knees giving way, her lovely body limp, spent. I heard her raw, soft sighing.

I stepped forward, turned her around, and enfolded her in my arms. Words were going to be useless for a while. She had no more cheerful obscenities for me. She huddled against my chest, and I felt the small kisses she dotted me with there. The night enveloped us and left us our tender moment of understanding and appreciation for this singular sexual act.

Fire and Ice

Leah Shannon

It's true, you know, they call me the Ice Queen. My coworkers don't know, though, how thoroughly their tough boss can melt when she's off the ice. That's fine with me, since tensions can run high at our remote research base high in an Alaskan ice field. Besides, in a way they're right, since I've been in love with the ice ever since my first cruise to Alaska many years ago. The incredible shades of blue, and the sounds of glaciers creaking and booming, captured my imagination and set me toward my career as a glaciologist. I've even wintered in Antarctica, but nothing has ever intruded on my love affair with the Alaskan ice.

Not even my long-standing relationship with Sven, who swears I fell in love with him because his eyes are that amazing deep turquoise blue of massively compacted glacial ice. They did indeed make me sit up and take notice, but the rest of my big blond polar bear isn't half bad, either. We don't see each other that often, but when we do we generate enough heat to boil the mighty Mendenhall. When I'm on the ice, Sven goes his own way, but we make up in intensity what we miss in continuity. For all my scientific detachment, I'm a raving hedonist at heart, and Sven is my chief indulgence.

Having recently returned from a research expedition, I was anxious to see Sven. After going through my usual routine of dumping my gear and filing my reports, I began making the necessary plans. I hopped a plane for Vancouver, which, if we have to have cities, is probably the finest in the world for climate, scenery, size, and civilization. You'd think Sven would meet me at the airport and whisk me away for a week of unadulterated passion, but I long ago decided that a little self-indulgent decompression time makes our reunions all the sweeter.

This was my time to pamper myself and transform the Ice Queen into the soft and yielding lover. A day at a shockingly expensive spa, with every conceivable lotion and potion, whirlpool, and massage didn't quite turn me into a cover girl, but it soothed my wind-burned skin, softened my hardworking hands, and let me relax by being pampered like a spoiled pussycat.

Sven collected me from the spa and took me off to his house on the north shore of the Straits. I curled into his arm and snuggled against his side as he drove, utterly content to mold my body to his. When we arrived, he helped me out of the car and swept me up into his arms, carrying me across the threshold as if I were a new bride. His house is fantastic, like something that grew out of the hillside, but I knew that most of what I would see of it for a while would be the huge, luxurious bedroom.

Its beamed ceiling seemed low only because Sven is so tall, and his bright hair and tanned face glowed like the rich wood hues of the walls and furniture. He lit the fire in the stone fireplace and rose to take me in his arms again and kiss me—a lingering, exploratory kiss, as if to see whether there was any unfamiliar taste or scent. His hands moved down my back and squeezed the cheeks of my ass, making me shiver with anticipatory delight. His voice rumbled in his chest like a calving glacier as he made his usual little joke about wanting to make sure it hadn't frozen over during all those weeks up north. I wriggled under his hands to demonstrate how thoroughly unfrozen I was, rubbing my pelvis into his crotch and feeling the familiar hardness of his cock against me. Damn, it was good to be home!

The fire caught, and its warm light bathed my skin as Sven pulled off my clothes, piece by piece, folding them neatly and placing them on the big leather chair. I let him turn me around like a doll and caress every part of my body before he bent to kiss my breasts, my belly, and the cheeks of my ass, the gentle abrasion of his mustache only adding to the heat rising within me.

Turning back around, I reached up and pulled his face down to mine, my lips and tongue hungry for his as my fingers tangled in his wiry hair. Inevitably, the moment came when I had to surface for air, and I stepped back reluctantly, but only far enough to let me unbutton his shirt and loosen the buckle of his belt. His trousers put up only token resistance to my shaking hands, and I peeled them down his muscular thighs until they were puddled around his feet. He kicked them aside, and I drew off his briefs, exposing the treasure they so inadequately hid.

The golden downy fur that covered his body erupted into

copper curls around his sex, framing his heavy balls. His cock was thick and sharply veined, its head the shape and color of a huge and succulent plum. Freed of its bonds, his shaft seemed to shake itself and rise to meet me. I took him in my hands and rubbed the lengthening shaft against my cheek, savoring its warmth and the softness that sheathed its steel. His masculine scent blended with the wood smoke to tantalize my senses.

Hefting his balls in my hand, I wrapped my fingers around his prick. Drawing its head across my face, I caressed it with my lips before opening them and lavishing licks on its sensitive velvet. When I gently prodded the tip of my tongue into the indentation of its slit, I could feel Sven shudder and moan.

Inch by inch, I fed his cock into my eager mouth, laving it until there was room for nothing more than the subtle movements I could manage with its weight lying on my tongue. I breathed deeply and began to hum as my throat opened to him. Letting him feel the vibrations of my larynx before I slid him out again, I began to repeat my action more swiftly until I was bobbing up and down on my prize like a woman possessed.

I felt him swell even more and was once again astonished that this prodigious organ could open my throat, my cunt, or my ass without splitting me altogether. Perhaps in a way it did, splitting open the icy carapace of my academic mind and revealing even to me the lusty warmth of my body.

He felt me shiver and knew very well that it had nothing to do with cold. Reaching down, he lifted me to my feet and held me close, grasping my buttocks in his hands and kneading them softly. "I missed you," he rumbled. "I think I didn't realize how much."

"I missed you, too," I replied as I kissed him and let him draw me up against his strong, warm body. His fingers probed my secret places from behind, discovering how wet and wanting I was, revealing my desires in every little moan and movement. He turned me so that my face was to the fire and my back and ass against him, his hardness resting in the cleft between my asscheeks as he lifted my breasts and rubbed my nipples between his blunt fingers. I melted against him, letting him play me like a cello, drawing out seemingly forgotten feelings, sending electric heat to curl and build throughout my body.

I rotated my ass against him, begging for what I knew we both loved best. The fantasy of shoving him down on his back and impaling myself on his rod raced through my mind, even as his strong hands clasped my waist and bent me over the warm, soft leather of the easy chair. I gave myself over to the paradox of forcing myself to yield to him what I most desired to have, and I sighed luxuriously as his fingers parted my buttocks, exposing the whole cleft of my sex to the fire-warmed air. I knew my cunt was glistening with evidence of my arousal, and I felt my asshole puckering involuntarily in its own plea to be invaded.

Sven took his time, making me crazy with a subtlety I could never quite convince him to abandon on these first nights. I wanted to be ravished, plowed, fucked brainless, all at once, but he made me wait. His thick fingers probed my cunt, drawing my natural lubricant back to coat the opening of my quivering ass. He parted my inner lips and drew his cockhead down over the mouth of my vagina, resting there a moment before rubbing hard against my clit, pulling a cry of need from my throat before he thrust a little way into me, coating his cockhead with my essence.

Another time I would have thrust back with my hips to try to take him into me, but I knew this was only the beginning of the delight I had longed and hungered for all these weeks.

Sven moved, drawing a line of wetness up to my puckered ass, and pressed his cock home. I let out an open-throated groan and relaxed every muscle at my command. He sank deep into my hungry flesh, opening the outer ring of muscle and waiting for the involuntary tightening that followed. I let him in even deeper, amazed at how perfectly the huge girth of his cock fit into that seemingly snug cavity. It stung a little at the edges as the first time always did, yet all that seemed to do was add a touch of spice to the roiling sex heat that penetrated to the depths of my heart.

I thought I had remembered how it felt, but I was wrong. As always, I had consoled myself with a pale shadow of reality. His cock slid deeper and deeper, making me wonder how my body could reconfigure its interior to accept such a prodigious length, and thankful that it could. I felt the wiry bush of his pubic hair against the smooth cheeks of my ass, and I let myself fall forward over the supporting back of the chair. Sven's hands caressed my flanks as he rested there a moment, fully sheathed in my palpitating ass.

This familiar pause wasn't meant as a contest, which was just as well since I always lost. Soon my ass was moving almost on its own, twisting and clenching against the axis of his cock, trying to entice him to do something. I knew how much he enjoyed this, having me fuck myself on his cock from sheer lust, but I knew that he'd be getting into the act soon. I pulled away a little, and sure enough his hands gripped my hips and pulled me back, initiating an escalating push-and-thrust that thrilled me to my core.

I gave myself over entirely to the delicious violence of it all, feeling his lean hips slam into the cheeks of my ass and my back door open to him as though astonished at his jackhammer ferocity. Then I felt a change, as though the smooth walls of my passage had been roughened by the friction of his urgent thrusts. It was as though my whole self were melting, heated to a viscous liquid that bathed his plunging shaft like warm oil.

His hand moved to my pussy, fumbling for a moment to find my opening. Then he touched the edge of my cunt and his thumb slid into my neglected orifice, his balled fist rubbing against my clit as he matched his thumb's thrusts to his cock's rhythm.

That was it; I could withstand no more, though I ached to prolong the exquisitely edgy sensation—the knife blade that separates orgasm from the unbearable. The hot tide within me crested and poured its tsunami through my veins. I washed along in its current, my ass and cunt contracting around the thicknesses that impaled them. I grabbed at something soft and found myself stuffing the sleeve of my sweater into my mouth to stifle my gasping howls of delight. My whole body shook as involuntary muscle spasms milked Sven's cock, making it feel even larger as his hips went rigid at the end of a final thrust and his hot seed rushed into me.

Sven bent over me, his cock still spurting a little into my convulsing ass, his breath hot on my ear, his strong arms holding me fast. We lay there over the chair back, panting, until his cock slipped out and he helped me upright. Turning me carefully to him, he kissed my slack and swollen lips and led me into the bathroom. He ran the shower, adjusting the hot spray before he helped me into it. We stood there under the deluge for a quiet, relaxing moment, then began to lather each other carefully, playfully but gently attentive to those tender parts so recently hard-used.

It was a sweet moment, our volcanic passion temporarily slaked. I treasured these quiet chances to savor the texture of his skin, the exquisite tone of his muscles, the pelt that covered his chest, and the golden-reddish down that covered his limbs. He soaped my body softly but thoroughly, using the hand spray to rinse me off before enfolding me in a huge fluffy bath sheet and patting me dry.

Sven guided me to the bed and tucked me in, padding down the stairs to the kitchen and returning a little later to rouse me from a delicious doze with a mug of hot chocolate laced with brandy. I sighed as he crawled in beside me and curved his body around mine, resting his own mug on my hip as I leaned back against him. We talked peacefully and drank our chocolate, setting aside our mugs for a cozy embrace that soon turned sexual when his cock stirred against my thigh.

This time I pushed him back against the pillows and took things in hand myself, stroking his cock to its full glory and reveling in its thickness and length. I kissed my prostrate lover and threw my leg across his hips, guiding his cock to the portal of my pussy and settling down around him slowly, moving carefully as this other part of my body adjusted to his size. I squeezed him with my inner muscles and rode him for a little while until the ache of desire in my ass rekindled and I let him go, but only for an instant. I loved the look of amazement in his dark ice-blue eyes as I redirected the arrow of his slickened prick to my only slightly loosened ass. There was something endearingly erotic about the way those beautiful eyes widened as I reached back and parted my asscheeks before holding his cock with one hand and lowering myself very deliberately upon it.

An incredible thrill shot through me, like and yet unlike the one that sang in my veins when I gave myself up to be ravished by my lover. This had a different edge, as though the act of self-impalement was more daring, more perversely sexual. For one thing, while it electrified every fiber of my being, I could not tell myself that I had been carried away by a power outside and beyond myself. That would happen shortly, but these studied moments made me take responsibility for my own lust in a way that was indescribably provocative.

Keeping my trajectory straight by placing my palms flat on Sven's chest, I let my weight drive his cock into my ass even deeper than our previous fucking had managed. Once his dick was seated in my depths, I sat up and parted my labia, displaying my swollen clit to my lover, brushing aside his hands as they reached to stroke my tender flesh. I ran two of my fingers across his lips, letting him suck them in and lick them with his tongue, a titillating oral caress. Withdrawing, I lowered my fingers to my clit and began to stroke myself, feeling that little nub of swollen flesh harden and heat beneath my fingertips, sending pulses of delight through my body and setting my ass aquiver.

I wanted to own this feeling in a way I never had before, and I took my time, sitting as still across his hips as a queen on her throne, yet tinglingly impaled on his rigid cock. The sensation built in my clitoris, soon reaching the breaking point. Its heat spread throughout my abdomen and the spasms started. Abandoning all restraint, I let Sven grab my hips and help me ride him wildly until we both came, his second torrent rushing into me moments before I collapsed across his heaving chest.

My ass twitched a little as his softening cock slid away, leaving it not nearly as bereft as it might have felt had we not fucked so hard before. I lay in his arms, spooning our bodies. Feeling his strength and warmth around me, I drifted off to sleep, his soft bass lullaby as comforting as the familiar creak of the ice so far away in that other wonderland where my heart had also found its home.

Wayward Traveler

Gavin Campanella

The motel where I work sits on a stretch of interstate highway out West, between nothing and nowhere. Our customers—bleary-eyed road warriors who stumble in after a stupefying day behind the wheel—just want to sleep for a few hours before resuming their journey. I'm the lucky guy who works the night shift at the front desk. I know that sounds sarcastic, but the truth is my luck really did come in one hot night last July.

It was around eleven p.m., and I was sitting in the air-conditioned stillness, lulled by the faint drone of seventy-five-mile-per-hour traffic on the interstate. I'd have been bored out of my mind if not for the copy of *Penthouse Variations* I was reading. Then came a blast of hot night air as the lobby door swooshed open, followed by the sound of approaching footsteps. I was so engrossed in my maga-zine that I didn't look up right away. When I did, my glance turned into a double take.

The woman standing before me belonged at a posh Beverly Hills hotel, not a crummy motor inn far from civilization. She looked a couple of years older than me, late twenties probably. The hair falling in lustrous curls about her face was darkly red. Her white sundress showed off her freckled shoulders and an ample amount of creamy cleavage. She smelled good, like she'd blown in on a fresh spring breeze from another world.

"Hi." She propped her elbows on the counter and leaned forward. "I'd like a room, please."

I tried to collect my wits. "Sure. Uh, fill this out." I slid the reservation form across the counter. Her eyes—sea-green irises rimmed with gold—lingered on me. Then she happened to glance down. Her eyes flicked back to my face almost at once, but now they twinkled mischievously. She'd seen what I was reading.

"Do you have a pen?" she asked, her smile growing more inter-esting by the minute. I handed her one. She tucked a strand of crimson hair behind her diamond-studded ear and put pen to paper with a quick, careless air. Thirty seconds later she handed the reservation form back to me, along with her credit card and driver's license.

Her name was Anna, and she was a long way from home. She'd listed her car as an Aston Martin convertible. *Yeah, right,* I thought. *No one who drove an Aston Martin would be caught dead in a joint like this.* Well, if she wanted to have a little fun with the details that was okay with me. I coded a key card and handed it over. As she took the key, Anna flashed me her hottest smile yet.

"P-park around the side," I stammered. "Your room's on the second floor."

Anna chuckled. "What's your name?"

"Gavin."

"Nice to meet you, Gavin."

With a parting wink, she headed for the door. I stood there admiring her perky ass and her sexy legs, which were bare to midthigh. Another blast of hot desert air hit me as the door opened. Then Anna was gone.

Feeling light-headed, I turned back to my magazine. I had a hard-on that wouldn't quit, and I was considering a retreat to the back office to relieve my condition when the phone rang. It was my most recent check-in calling.

"How can I help you, Ms.—?"

"Oh, I love the sound of that, Gavin. You're the first one to say it in five years. But call me Anna. Have you got any glassware? I'd rather not drink champagne from a plastic cup."

"Sure…Anna. We have glasses in the breakfast room. I'll bring one over."

"Bring two," she said. "Thanks, Gavin."

I hung up the phone and put the WILL RETURN SHORTLY sign on the counter. Then I got the glasses and headed for Anna's room.

It was still quite warm outside, despite the hour. "Come in," Anna called when I knocked on her door. Inside, the ancient air conditioner rattled away, to minimal effect. The shag carpeting and low ceiling screamed 1970s. The scene was all pretty shabby.

"Here are your glasses," I called out, letting the door close behind me. Anna's suitcase was in the corner, but she herself was not in sight. Light spilled from the doorway to the small bathroom. I peeked in and there she was, in the tub, with bubbles up to her slender neck.

"Wonderful," Anna said, beaming at me. "There's the champagne. Have a glass with me."

I thought about the front desk, unattended. I thought about what my boss would say. Then I grabbed the bottle from the ice bucket, popped the cork, and filled both glasses. Handing one to Anna, I asked, "What are we celebrating?"

As she lifted her arm from the suds to take her glass, a goodly portion of her right breast came into view. "My divorce," she replied. "I finally got the papers this morning." She took a sip of bubbly and went on, "Michael's a good man, but we were never right for each other. He let me have the Aston Martin. I put the pedal to the metal and haven't looked back."

So she hadn't been joking about the car. I had other things to think about, though, because Anna was rising from the bathwater like Aphrodite from the sea. She paused to down the rest of her champagne and then handed the empty glass to me. Clinging bubbles hid her private parts, but not for long; Anna slid her hands over her shiny-wet body, wiping the suds off. Truly nude now, she stepped out of the tub with brazen assurance. My cock was already as hard as wood, on its way to forged steel.

"Towel, please?" Anna said.

I grabbed one for her. She used it on her hair, taking her time. Handing it back to me, she turned and said, "Dry my back?"

I put my glass down, took a deep breath, and started at her shoulders. I was about halfway to the enticing swell of her ass when she whirled around to face me. Startled, I dropped the towel. Her breasts were large yet surprisingly buoyant; her nipples stiffened as they brushed against my hands. Anna stepped closer, pressing herself against me from hip to chest. When she lifted her pretty mouth for a kiss, I was ready. Circling her waist with my arm, I pressed my lips to hers. She sucked my lower lip into her mouth; our tongues danced madly.

"It's incredible," I said, "to think I met you only an hour ago."

"Less than that," Anna said, "but who's counting? I never count, Gavin. I just follow my desires."

She darted out of the bathroom and threw herself across the bed. I followed while tugging my polo shirt off—and then stopped, transfixed. Anna reclined on the bed in all her naked glory, with her still-damp hair fanned out across a mound of white pillows. Her breasts were like mouth-watering cones of vanilla ice cream, complete with cherries on top. Her midriff was toned and slim, and her long legs were carelessly splayed, revealing the smooth lips of her pussy. My gaze was arrested by Anna's artfully groomed pubic mound. It was diamond-shaped and close cropped—like a putting green—but most striking of all was its fiery red color. The effect against her alabaster skin was striking.

I dropped my shirt on the floor and got on the bed, straddling Anna. We kissed again, passionately, while her hands raked my back and mine played with her boobs. She was breathing heavily by the time I moved downward to kiss her breasts. She arched her back off the bed, and I licked and sucked her nipples, making her gasp. I slid one hand down along her side to stroke her hip, while I used the other to massage her breasts. Anna began to make soft, deep-rooted sounds of pleasure; her whole body thrummed beneath me like a finely tuned racing engine.

After petting and suckling at her exquisite breasts a while longer, I revved her up even more by continuing down her belly to between her legs. She reached for my head with a kind of primal moan, anticipating my next move. I lowered my face between her creamy thighs, and my nostrils filled with the heady scent of her arousal. Anna's skin, dewy-fresh from the bath, was as smooth as a rose leaf. I wished I'd taken more care with my shave that morning, because it seemed a crime to rub my stubbly face against the incredible softness of her inner thighs. She craved it, though; with a shudder of desire she drew me in farther, to her most sensitive flesh. I kissed her smooth pussy lips and pushed my tongue between them, exploring her juicy folds. With a sound like the coo of a dove, Anna coiled her fingers in my hair and held me aggressively to her hot spot. I parted her outer lips with two fingers and lapped away, paying special attention to her clit. Before I knew it, she was squirming wildly and bucking against my face. I sealed my mouth to her opening and kept at it, relishing the taste and succulence of her inner recesses.

"Jesus, Gavin… Oh yeah, baby," cried Anna, as her pussy moistened my lips and chin with its sweet honey. Her thighs clamped to my ears, and she shook mightily with the force of her climax. When at last she released me, it was only to get at the zipper of my pants and yank it down. My cock was aching by then, of course, so I got my shoes, pants, and underwear off in record time.

Anna turned herself over on hands and knees and looked back at me, inviting me to mount her from the rear. As I moved to get in position, she dropped her shoulders all the way to the mattress, leaving her backside high in the air. The impatient girl rocked back at me. "Come on, Gavin," she intoned, her face turned sideways on the pillow. "Put your dick in me. I want to feel you deep inside."

Kneeling behind Anna's sexy ass, I took firm hold of her hips, nuzzled my cockhead between her swollen cunt lips, and pushed inside. The warm, creamy depths of her pussy almost made me swoon.

Anna was completely focused on the feeling of my heavy pole as it filled her up. When I bottomed out, she gave a long, pleasurable sigh and slowly, rhythmically, began to rock against me. I stroked the sides of her ass and moved with her. As we bumped together, I had the added visual treat of seeing my fat shaft disappear into and reappear from Anna's juicy hole again and again. I saw her fingers down there, too, as Anna reached back and started playing with her clit from below. Pounding her faster, I slapped her ass a couple of times, hard enough to leave a momentary pink outline of my hand on her white skin. "Oh!" she cried, rocking ever more violently to meet my thrusts. Her fingers were working furiously at her clit, and I was slamming my cock in and out of her cunt sharply enough to make the bed bang against the wall. With a long, high-pitched squeal, she came like a hellcat. I felt the gush of her molten pussy all along the length of my cock. Even my ball sac dampened as it slapped against her slick labia. She kept right on fucking me, frenetically seesawing on her elbows and knees to draw out our mutual pleasure as long as possible. She was on a mission to extract the cream from my balls, and she soon succeeded. With a mighty grunt, I pushed up against her one last time, pulled out, and deposited my load all over her ass. The spurts kept coming and coming, until finally I sat back, panting. Anna whirled around and, fixing me briefly with a wicked grin, licked my cock clean.

I flopped back on the bed. Anna went into the bathroom for a minute, then came back, turned off the lights, and lay down on the bed beside me. Eventually, her slow, even breathing told me she was asleep, and I dozed off, too. I had a really nice dream of a beautiful redhead going down on me, worshipping my cock with her eager mouth. The sense of her soft lips and velvety tongue sliding up and down my manhood was so deliciously real that I woke up with a start, and discovered I wasn't dreaming.

I don't know how long we'd been asleep—a couple of hours, maybe—but the room was still dark, except for a narrow shaft of moonlight coming through the curtains. The bluish-white beam fell across the bed and gleamed in Anna's hair as she bobbed up and down, hungrily sucking my dick. I was pretty hard already, and when I looked down at the awesome sight of Anna's rapacious antics, my erection quickly maxed out. Realizing that I'd awakened, she glanced up and met my gaze. Her mouth was sloppy, and her eyes gleamed with desire. She licked her lips and went back to work on my cock with even more glee than before. I smiled to myself in the dark, marveling at Anna's insatiable lust.

My cock throbbed as she swirled her tongue around and around my sensitive crown. Meanwhile, her hand played with my balls, expertly massaging them in a way that made me moan. Spurred on by my reaction, she ran her tongue down there and thoroughly laved my balls while she pumped her hand up and down my prick. Then she moved even lower. My eyes widened as she tongued my back hole and dipped a finger in there. Waves of pleasure rolled through me; I was in the hands of a master. Returning once more to my cock, Anna sucked my sensitive organ so ardently that I'd have shot my load down her throat in another minute. She realized this, too, and decided to change things up, anxious to keep me on the edge a while longer.

Shooting me a wonderfully devilish look, Anna climbed on top of me and squatted over my shaft. Her hand went down past her russet pubes, and her fingers splayed the folds of her pussy as she centered herself over my cock's portly crest. Then, with a quivering sound of anticipation, she lowered her body and speared herself on my lengthy rod. She was sopping wet inside. As her pale, lithe frame settled against my groin, her eyes fluttered closed; she seemed momentarily overcome by the depth of pleasure she was experiencing. Her fingers were still in motion, touching herself near where my cock disappeared inside her before she brought all of her weight to bear against me. She was trembling with excitement, and she pivoted her hips this way and that, rubbing her clit against my root. Finally, her eyes opened; she gave me a sly look and brought her hand to my lips, giving me a taste of her wetness. I sucked her fingers into my mouth, making her grin with salacious delight.

The shaft of moonlight from the window fell now across Anna's breasts. I reached out and stroked those ivory mounds, drawing a moan of delight from my companion when I fingered her erect nipples. I let my touch wander down her sides to her supple, curving hips. Reaching back farther, I squeezed her ass.

Anna began to move like a piston atop my cock. She rose, fell, rose, and fell again, her hips and thighs flexing as she rode my pole. The mattress springs began to squeak as her pace increased. Leaning forward over me, she took my hands in hers and held them to the bed on either side of my head. "Relax," she purred, "and let me fuck you."

I was happy to comply, at least for the moment. Lying still

beneath Anna, I relished her enthusiasm as she rutted and rocked with my steel-hard cock inside her. I could not, however, resist the temptation to lick her heavenly boobs, given their immediate proximity to my mouth. My efforts made Anna even wilder. She rode my penis with an abandon that took my breath away. I thrust my cock into her from below, wondering how much longer I could hold out.

Then—in the darkness I couldn't see this well, but I certainly felt it—Anna lifted off me for the briefest of moments, just enough to reach down and replant my spike at her smaller, tighter hole. It was a surprisingly minute adjustment, and Anna performed it with well-practiced finesse, but I could feel the change at once—the tight yet elastic grip of her back door as it yielded to the entrance of my juice-slickened cock. In just a few seconds, my crown was through her ring of muscle and into the enveloping space beyond.

"Oh…oh yeah," Anna whispered as she sank down, taking my slippery dick farther into her ass. "Oh my god—yes…" She bottomed out, her asscheeks nestling against my balls. It was the most incredible feeling to be all the way in there, filling up her rear passage. Once acclimated, Anna resumed her lusty pace, only now she sat up straight and rode me with her hands on her thighs. Her firm breasts bounced only a little, but her hair flew in every direction and her cries of passion filled the room. It wasn't long before I reached the point of no return. With a throaty cry of my own, I jacked my hips off the bed and climaxed, shooting gobs of hot cream into Anna's ass. I guess my violent orgasm tripped Anna's hot-wire, too. She sat down hard and ground herself against me, shuddering and moaning uncontrollably. Her anus clenched, and I felt her pussy drench everything below it in sticky wetness.

After catching our breath, we enjoyed a quick shower together, and then we returned to the bed and slept deeply. At least I did—deeply enough to miss Anna's departure. It was well past dawn when I woke up. Anna and her suitcase were gone, but she'd left me a note: *Thanks for an unforgettable start to the rest of my life.* I smiled and silently wished her safe travels.

www.ingramcontent.com/pod-product-compliance
Lightning Source LLC
Chambersburg PA
CBHW010447100726

47904CB00008B/2504